I0760672

Exploring Dark Short Fiction #3: A Primer to Nisi Shawl

Exploring Dark Short Fiction (A Primer Series)
Created by Eric J. Guignard

#1: A Primer to Steve Rasnic Tem (Dark Moon Books, 2017)

#2: A Primer to Kaaron Warren (Dark Moon Books, 2018)

#3: A Primer to Nisi Shawl (Dark Moon Books, 2018)

#4: A Primer to Jeffrey Ford (Dark Moon Books, 2019)

#5: A Primer to Han Song (Dark Moon Books, 2020)

#6: A Primer to Ramsey Campbell (forthcoming) (Dark Moon Books, 2020)

Fiction Written by Eric J. Guignard

Doorways to the Deadeye (JournalStone, 2019)

Last Case at a Baggage Auction (Harper Day Books, 2020)

That Which Grows Wild: 16 Tales of Dark Fiction (Cemetery Dance Publications, 2018)

Anthologies Edited by Eric J. Guignard

A World of Horror (Dark Moon Books, 2018)

After Death... (Dark Moon Books, 2013)

Dark Tales of Lost Civilizations (Dark Moon Books, 2012)

The Five Senses of Horror (Dark Moon Books, 2018)

+Horror Library+ Volume 6 (Cutting Block Books/ Farolight Publishing, 2017)

Pop the Clutch: Thrilling Tales of Rockabilly, Monsters, and Hot Rod Horror (Dark Moon Books, 2019)

The Horror Writers Association Presents: Haunted Library of Horror Classics
Edited by Eric J. Guignard and Leslie S. Klinger

Vol. I: The Phantom of the Opera by Gaston Leroux (Sourcebooks, 2020)

Vol. II: The Beetle by Richard Marsh (Sourcebooks, 2020)

Vol. III: Vathek by William Beckford (Sourcebooks, 2020)

Vol. IV: The House on the Borderland by William Hope Hodgson (forthcoming) (Sourcebooks, 2020)

Vol. V: The Parasite and Other Tales of Terror by Arthur Conan Doyle (forthcoming) (Sourcebooks, 2021)

Vol. VI: The King in Yellow by Robert W. Chambers (forthcoming) (Sourcebooks, 2021)

Exploring Dark Short Fiction #3: A Primer to Nisi Shawl

Edited by Eric J. Guignard
Commentary by Michael Arnzen, PhD
Illustrations by Michelle Prebich

Dark Moon Books
Los Angeles, California

EXPLORING DARK SHORT FICTION #3: A PRIMER TO NISI SHAWL

Edited by Eric J. Guignard
Interior layout by Eric J. Guignard
Cover design by Eric J. Guignard
www.ericjguignard.com

Commentary by Michael Arnzen, PhD
www.gorelets.com

Interior illustrations by Michelle Prebich
www.batinyourbelfry.etsy.com

"The Beads of Ku" © 2002 by Nisi Shawl. First published in *Rosebud #23*, April, Rosebud, Inc.
"Otherwise" © 2012 by Nisi Shawl. First published in *Brave New Love: 15 Dystopian Tales of Desire*, edited by Paula Guran, Running Press.
"Just Between Us" © 2011by Nisi Shawl. First published in *Phantom Drift, A Journal of New Fabulism #1*, Fall, Phantom Drift Limited.
"At the Huts of Ajala" © 2000 by Nisi Shawl. First published in *Dark Matter: A Century of Speculative Fiction from the African Diaspora*, edited by Sheree R. Thomas, Aspect/ Warner Books.
"Street Worm" © 2014 by Nisi Shawl. First published in *Streets of Shadows*, edited by Maurice Broaddus and Jerry Gordon, Alliteration Ink.
"Written On The Water" © 2010 by Nisi Shawl. First published in *The Aqueduct Gazette #7*, Spring/Summer, Aqueduct Press.

First edition published in December, 2018
Library of Congress Control Number: 2018932288
ISBN-13: 978-1-949491-09-8 (hardback)
ISBN-13: 978-0-9989383-4-9 (paperback)
ISBN-13: 978-0-9989383-5-6 (e-book)

DARK MOON BOOKS
Los Angeles, California
www.DarkMoonBooks.com
Made in the United States of America

(V061520)

This book is dedicated to those who encourage the written word, those who seek a deeper understanding of literature, and those who simply love dark fiction.

And of course, this is dedicated also to Nisi Shawl, an inspiration to so many. Thank you for consenting to this project.

Table of Contents

Introduction

by Eric J. Guignard

THIS IS THE THIRD VOLUME IN THE SERIES *Exploring Dark Short Fiction* and, like raising children, it has become my favorite in different ways from its siblings. The stories of Nisi Shawl straddle the amorphous bounds between the world we live and the world(s) we *could* live, alternately presenting views of both dark dystopian and hopeful utopian scenes, or simply offering an alternate view to *today*. Her writing speaks to societal issues and to philosophy, and to political activism and global awareness, to issues of culture and history and identity, all the while wrapping her messages within an invigorating artistic prowess of beauty, whim, and fantasy.

Or, more succinctly, Nisi pushes the boundaries of meaningful fiction, to the benefit of us all.

In 2016, The Washington Post wrote of Nisi's work (*Everfair*): "...It's a tribute to Shawl's powerful writing that her intricate, politically and racially charged imaginary world seems as believable—sometimes more believable—than the one we inhabit."

In this, I find the essence of Nisi's collected output, a sense of believability that no matter how fantastic the setting or situation, it allows me to consider, *This could happen.*

Case in point: One of my favorite stories of Nisi's is "The Pragmatical Princess," in which a French-speaking dragon is converted to Muslim by a captive princess for the most pragmatic of reasons. In only a 4,600-word story, the author discusses differences in ancient culture, doctrine, and eastern religion, while also painting a remarkable setting and relationship between characters. And the plot: Regardless how implausible the storyline, to me it makes complete sense. It's reasonable, and it's *beautiful.* It's Fantasy with a message, with significance. It's Nisi Shawl, and it speaks to her savvy.

Another example is "Vulcanization," which is a tie-in to her novel, *Everfair*, and a haunting characterization of Leopold II, king of Belgium, who is historically atrocious for his exploitation and genocide of millions of native Congolese while pursuing personal riches via the lucrative rubber trade. Herein is an alternate view to history, and a steampunk one at that, filled with murky mechanizations and the tragic maimed ghosts of Leopold's own reign, torturing him with sights of what his violent subjugations have wrought. As somber as "The Pragmatical Princess" is hopeful, "Vulcanization" nonetheless humanizes a despot, while speaking to issues of racism and colonialism, and also the human emotions of guilt, of fear, of disgrace. Again, it's Fantasy with a message, and again, it speaks to Nisi's savvy.

And there are so many more! Although I did not include the above mentioned stories within this Primer, there are six others, and in each selection Nisi's distinctive voice and message shines through in ways that are sometimes inspiring, sometimes grim, yet always complex and satisfying. Whether speaking to ideas such as empowerment in "At the Huts of Ajala"; love and multicultural unity in "Otherwise"; or sexual identification and liberation in "Conversion Therapy," Nisi finds way to *connect* and to nurture the reader.

And perhaps her avid perceptions are due to life experiences, for vast exposure to those around us leads to vast understanding, and there is little that Nisi has not done or been involved with in the literary realm since auspicious leanings away from college (where she began at only age 16), and into a sort of artists' colony for immersion into writing, art, and discourse, of which—in the early 1970s—sounds like an exquisite culmination of what I imagine as the ideals of a young bohemian lifestyle. By now, it seems, attempting to label Nisi as *only* an author or writer would seem too constrictive, as she is involved with any number of other tangential belletristic callings.

Praised by literary journals, news outlets, and leading fiction magazines, Nisi Shawl is tirelessly celebrated as an author whose works are lyrical and philosophical, speculative and far-ranging; "... broad in ambition and deep in accomplishment" (*The Seattle Times*). Besides nearly three decades of creating fantasy and science fiction, fairy tales, and indigenous stories, Nisi has also been lauded as editor, journalist, reviewer, teacher, speaker, afrofuturist, and proponent and mentor of feminism, African-American fiction, and other pedagogical issues of diversity.

And now she is here in this third Primer. So whether, dear reader, you are a first time visitor to Nisi's worlds, or else a fan wishing to learn more of her merit, consider that while her messages may wind in surprising directions, growing to beautifully intricate constructions, my message is quite simple: *Read Nisi Shawl.*

Midnight cheers,

—Eric J. Guignard
Chino Hills, California
October 31, 2018

About Nisi Shawl

MY LIFE

WHEN I WAS LITTLE, I TOLD MY MIDDLE SISTER Julie convoluted tales of how I, a mermaid, had come to dwell in the small Midwestern town of Kalamazoo, Michigan. This odyssey involved the Saint Lawrence Seaway, several of the Great Lakes, and mysterious underground passages my schoolteacher called aquifers. Her own origin was much simpler, of course; our parents, I explained, had found her in a garbage can.

At sixteen, in 1971, I moved from Kalamazoo to Ann Arbor to attend the University of Michigan's Residential College. I took several French courses, Oral History, Cosmology, and a poetry seminar that taught me ten weeks of nothing. Most classes took place in the dorm, and I got a job in the dorm's library. One day I was startled to notice an extremely short person walking toward me. They were less than two feet high. It took me several seconds to realize that this was a child.

Anyone under a certain age had become alien to my experience. It wasn't this isolation that led to my dropping out of school. I had an abortion. I became depressed. I quit going to classes two weeks from finals. I failed to finish my assignments, and left the University without a degree.

I moved into a house called Cosmic Plateau and lived with people who called themselves Bozoes. I paid $65 a month rent. I worked part-time as a janitor, an au pair, a dorm cook, an artists' model. I wrote. I performed my writings publicly, at parks and cafes and museums. I learned a lot.

I read Charnas, Russ, Delany, Colette, Wittig. I sent out a horrible story about fornicating centaurs and got a wonderfully sweet rejection letter. Then our landlady kicked all the Bozoes out of Cosmic Plateau, and I had to live by the sweat of my brow.

I worked at a natural foods warehouse. I sold structural steel and aluminum. I sold used books. I got married. I joined a band.

I kept writing. I got better.

My first science fiction appearance was in the nude. I modeled for one of Rick Lieder's illustrations for Bruce Sterling's *Crystal Express* (the Arkham House hardcover—I'm the Dark Girl of "Telliamed").

My first science fiction publication was in *Semiotext(e)* (see my bibliography for dates on this and the rest of my print oeuvre). I shared the table of contents with William S. Burroughs, J.G. Ballard, Bruce Sterling, William Gibson, and a bunch of less well-known but quite cool others. I owe my part in this literary conspiracy to Crowbar, publisher of the 'zine *Popular Reality*.

In 1992 I attended a cyberpunk "symposium" in Detroit. Sterling, in his inimitable manner, supposed that no one in the audience had heard of *Semiotext(e)*, let alone read it, and I was able to retort from the third row that I was *in* it. So I got to hang out with him, and with Pat Cadigan and John Shirley, which last professional offered to *read my stories*! He was of the opinion that I could write. He recommended that I attend the Clarion West Writers' Workshop, where he and Cadigan were to teach that summer.

At Clarion West I learned in six weeks what six years at the University could never have taught me.

Because of Clarion West and another writers' program in the Puget Sound area (Cottages at Hedgebrook, a retreat on Whidbey

Island), I put Seattle near the top of my list when considering a move from Michigan. I'd gotten divorced. We'd sold the house. When I asked my ancestors where I ought to live, they said this was the place.

My apartment is one block off of the #48 bus route. King County Metro takes me all the way to the beach. Gray and wild, or smooth as oil, the water is unfailingly beautiful. By ways as circuitous as those I described to my sister almost four decades ago, this mermaid has returned to the sea.

A BIOGRAPHY

NISI SHAWL'S DOZENS OF ACCLAIMED STORIES have appeared in *Analog* and *Asimov's* Magazines and in anthologies ranging from the groundbreaking *Dark Matter* series to Salon's online *Trump Project*, among many other publications. Her story "Vulcanization" was selected as one of twenty offered in Houghton Mifflin Harcourt's *Best American Science Fiction and Fantasy*. Though best known for her short fiction, Shawl wrote the 2016 Nebula finalist and Tiptree Honor novel *Everfair*, an alternate history in which the Congo overthrows King Leopold II's genocidal regime. *Everfair* was hailed by Karen Joy Fowler as "luminous" and "original," a "wonderful achievement." Ursula K. Le Guin described Shawl's 2008 Tiptree Award-winning short story collection *Filter House* as "superbly written."

In 2005, Shawl co-wrote *Writing the Other: A Practical Approach* with Cynthia Ward. This book is now considered the standard text on diverse character representation in the imaginative genres, and it forms the basis of her years of online and in-person classes offered under the same name. She is a founder of the inclusivity-focused Carl Brandon Society and has served on the Clarion West Writers Workshop's board of directors for nineteen years.

Since the turn of the millennium, Shawl has reviewed books for *The Seattle Times*, her local daily newspaper. She also occasionally freelances reviews for *Ms. Magazine*, *The Washington Post*, and *The Los Angeles Review of Books*. She contributes monthly columns to *The Seattle Review of Books* and to *Tor.com*—the latter column expanding on her seminal 2016 "Crash Course in the History of Black Science Fiction" essay.

Shawl edits the reviews section of the feminist literary quarterly *The Cascadia Subduction Zone*. In the past she has edited and co-edited several fiction and nonfiction anthologies such as *Stories for Chip: A Tribute to Samuel R. Delany*; and *Strange Matings: Science Fiction, Feminism, African American Voices, and Octavia E. Butler*; both finalists for the Locus Award. Currently she's in the final stages of editing *New Suns: Original Speculative Fiction by People of Color*, to be published in March 2019 by Solaris Books.

She lives in Seattle, near a lake with enticingly strong currents, and takes frequent walks through the neighborhood with her mother June and her cat Minnie, at the pace of an entitled feline.

The Beads of Ku

THERE WAS A WOMAN NAMED DOSI, AND SHE GAVE birth to twins. At first both were weak and sickly, but the boy died, and then the girl prospered and grew strong. She was a good girl, willing to work hard, and with good sense.

When she was still very young, Fulla Fulla helped her mother in the market, running messages for her and bringing her the news. "Mother," she would say, "the women of Dit-ao-lane are over by the baobab, looking for cloth to make beautiful robes. Quick, give me that basket of feathers, that I may tempt them with bright colors." And Fulla Fulla would run to the river and sell all the feathers very dear. Or she would return from an errand leading a row of porters bearing salt. "Mother," she would say, "I have traded all our leather for this salt, and I got it very cheap. The merchant did not want to take it on with him and pay another duty. He did not know that in two days the taxes will be lowered because the King himself will be trading his salt for a new shipment of gold from the South . . ." And this was when Fulla Fulla was just a little girl.

As the woman Dosi grew older, she began more and more to stay at home and to leave all the business to Fulla Fulla. At last she became ill, and though Fulla Fulla nursed her mother diligently, she died. Fulla Fulla grieved for her mother, but she did not let grief make her weak or stupid. Those who tried to take advantage of her state soon found that this was so. It was harder than ever to read her face beneath the gray ashes of mourning. And though her eyes were red and filled with tears, they missed nothing. So Fulla Fulla kept her place in the market and did well.

One day as she walked in the market she passed by the stall of a hunter selling cooked meat. "If I buy all your meat," she asked him, "will you give it to me for such-and-such a price?" The price she named was very low.

The hunter was a simple man, not a trader, and he sold the meat to her at the price that she had named. Then she took all that she had bought to the other side of the market and sold it for many times the price she had paid.

The next market day the hunter was there again, and she did the same thing. But the time after that he was not there. When he came again she asked him why he had not come to the last market. He said, "I hate to come to the city, where there are so many people, and noises, and ugly smells. I knew it was the market day, but I could not bear to leave the savannah. Besides, I was sure that you would buy all my meat, whenever I brought it." And he shrugged his big strong shoulders.

This gave Fulla Fulla an idea. "Come to my house," she said, "and I will fix you a fine meal from your own meat." The hunter was happy to hear this. He had lost his first wife many years ago, and he had not had a really fine meal since. He ate up everything Fulla Fulla cooked. When they were alone, he made her his wife.

For a while, the hunter and Fulla Fulla were very happy together. He stayed out on the savannah, hunting as long as he liked. When he wanted to, he came into the city and had a fine meal. He brought her all his meat, and she sold it in the market for a good price, and they prospered and grew very rich. But one market day, the hunter came to the city and Fulla Fulla was not there. He sent messengers all through the market. None found her. Angry and worried, the hunter stayed in the house. He did not know what to do. He felt helpless, and also he did not like to spend so much time cramped up in town. But just as he was getting ready to give up, his wife walked in the door. "Where have you been?" he started to ask her. Then he noticed that she was wearing at her ears a certain kind of bead, called "the Beads of Ku." Then he knew that she had been to the Marketplace of Death.

When she heard that she had missed the market day, Fulla Fulla was upset. "Time has cheated me!" she said. "I spent only a little while there, but you say I have been gone for days. This must not be so." She frowned in heavy thought. "I will ask my mother what to do."

At these words the hunter's stomach grew cold with fear, and he tried to dissuade his wife from going again to Ku.

But Fulla Fulla looked at him fondly. "You are a fine, great, man," she said. "But you have no understanding of business at all. Of course I will go there again." And she set about planning her next trip.

The hunter returned to the savannah. He killed an antelope and two duikers. He saw many beautiful and restful sights, but he was ill at ease.

When he returned to the house he found Fulla Fulla there. Again she had missed a market day, but this time she did not seem so concerned. "It's easy what we must do," she said. She handed him a little whistle. "You must always return to town a day before market and blow upon this whistle. Then I will be called back." Good.

So the hunter did as Fulla Fulla told him to do, and they were happy. But not so happy as before. Now he could not spend as much time hunting as he wished. He had to come back to the city every three days, to blow the whistle and call his wife from the Market of Death.

Also, it seemed as if his wife was becoming a little strange. She had strange ideas, and she knew things one should not know, from talking to dead people. Whenever there was no one else around to see, she wore the Beads of Ku.

She boasted to her husband of her dealings with the dead. "Those of Ku want very simple things," she said. "For yams and cassava, they will trade ornaments of ivory! If I were a camel, I could carry enough goods to make us richer than the King himself."

"Why would a camel want to be rich?" he asked. Fulla Fulla laughed.

She spoke much of her mother and her doings, and of her twin brother, Kinsu. The hunter felt she spoke too much of these dead people. "I am her husband," he said to himself. "Her thoughts should be of me." When he spoke like this to himself, he remembered his first wife, Agbanli.

Agbanli had thought only of him and how to make him happy. She had never laughed at him or known strange things one should not know. She had never gone to Ku until properly dead.

Thinking like this made the hunter think more. He wondered what it was like in Ku and if Agbanli was happy there, or if she missed him. He wondered how Fulla Fulla went there and came back again. He wondered if he would be able to go and return, and if he might see Agbanli there and comfort her.

One day the hunter told Fulla Fulla that he was going out on the savannah. But he went only to the edge of the city and waited until it was dark. Then he went back to his house and hid himself nearby. Toward morning, his wife emerged from the house. The hunter followed her. She walked out of the city to the west. She walked for a long way, till she came to a cave in a hillside. A river flowed out of the cave and down the hill. Without stopping a moment, Fulla Fulla threw herself into the river. You would think that she would drown, but instead she was carried away quickly by the water. In an instant she was gone from his sight.

The hunter stood on the bank. He tossed a stick into the water. The water carried it away, but in the way a river normally carries away a stick. It did not just disappear, like Fulla Fulla.

"Something is very strange here," said the hunter. "But I already knew that." And he flung himself into the river, after his wife.

It seemed as though no time at all passed before he found himself in Ku. The river, which before had been like a strong wind blowing him on, became suddenly wet. He pulled himself from the water and up onto the bank. Fulla Fulla had already left for the Market, and he was surrounded by dead people he did not know. They looked sad and tired. He asked for Agbanli, his first wife, but when they saw he had no Beads, they would not speak to him. They only glanced at him and walked away.

He found his way to the Marketplace of Death. Wonderful goods were displayed there: lengths of cloth spun from gold, ivory carved into chairs and canopies, and many other marvelous things. But everyone was crowded at one end of the Market, trying to buy the goods at one little stall. "That must be Fulla Fulla's stall," thought the hunter. He was curious to see what she had brought, so he went closer.

Just then, the King of Ku came into the Marketplace. The hunter knew this was the King from the magnificence of his progress. Two giants went before him, beating on copper drums. Two dwarves came after them and swept the dust from the King's path. The King walked in splendid robes covered in strange jewels that shone with their own light. Everyone bowed respectfully to the ground and made a path for him. The hunter watched fearfully as the King of Death began trading with his wife. He hoped he would not be noticed.

The King offered a string of rubies for a package of Arabian raisins. Fulla Fulla was not satisfied. She wanted more. The King offered her a delicate chain carved from a single piece of ebony, but he demanded that she include a jar of honey and three figs. The hunter began to sweat. Fulla Fulla asked the King if he had any diamonds. She was agreeable as to the honey, but she positively had to have a large diamond for each and every fig. The King looked offended. He turned away as if to leave. The hunter could stand no more.

"Stop!" he shouted. "Fulla Fulla, what are you thinking of? He is the *King of Death*! *Sell* him all your goods, take whatever he will give, and *leave*!"

Fulla Fulla looked at him and screamed. "You, here? Oh, fool, you have ruined us. Truly, you have no understanding of business at all."

The King, too, was very angry. "Fulla Fulla," he said, "you have broken our agreement. You were forbidden to bring anyone, or even to speak of our transactions. Yet here is this living man, here where no man living should be. He calls you by name. You call him a fool. Can you deny that he is here because of you?"

The King of Ku was really most upset. He could keep Fulla Fulla here with him, and her raisins, and the honey and figs now, as well. But these would be the last.

Fulla Fulla was looking at her husband, and her heart softened as her eyes took in his beauty. She thought fondly of the many warm nights that they had spent together and how well he had provided her with meat. Also she thought how fearless he was and how much he must love her to come after her to Ku. She did not know about Agbanli. She only knew that though he was a fool, he was a brave one, and for that she loved him. But she did not let love make her weak or stupid. She thought quickly and made up her mind how to deal with the King of Death.

"Yes, King, what you say is all too true," admitted Fulla Fulla. "He is my husband, and an excellent provider of meat. He would have been most happy to hunt for you, and to bring you fresh antelope, and smoked duiker. But now you must keep us here and punish us both, and so you will get nothing."

"It is not for *you* to decide these things," flared the King. "*I* am the one who decrees how justice will best be served. I will retire and consider what must be done." And he withdrew to the far side of the Market, to think of fat pumpkins and savory stews.

Fulla Fulla knew what was in his mind. She took aside the hunter and spoke with him alone. "The King will give you two Beads," she said. "Accept them, and thank him. But you must never use them. As he sends you back, let the Beads fall from your hands. You must never come here again in your life. I am afraid that if *you* tried to trade with the King of Ku, you would die long before your time."

Then the King beckoned to them, and they came before him. "This is how it will be," said the King. "Fulla Fulla must stay here. She gave her word, and her word was no good. But you, hunter, may come and go as she has done. Whenever you come you must be sure to bring me your own weight in meat, and any other good things I ask you to get for me." He smiled and held out his open hand. "Take these. They will allow you to return to the living when you wish. They are proof that I am no longer angry with you."

As the hunter took the Beads, he felt as if many things were just beginning to come clear to him. The faces of all the dead people became familiar. He thought he saw Agbanli in the crowd, though she looked different than he remembered. She looked as though she were about to speak. But the King made a sign with his hand, and then the hunter flung the Beads away, as he had been told to do.

Suddenly, he found himself at home. The sun was rising. It was morning, the same morning on which he had left.

At first he thought he had fallen asleep and dreamt his visit to Ku. He wandered through the house looking for Fulla Fulla. He wanted to tell her about his strange dream. But she was not there. And she never came back again, though he blew and blew upon the little whistle.

The Beads of Ku: A Commentary

TOLD AS TRUE AS A COLONIAL AFRICAN FOLKTALE, "The Beads of Ku" is a story about a woman's abilities to wheel and deal in the "Marketplace of Death" in a quest for wealth to bring back to her husband, the hunter. Fulla Fulla is an artful negotiator and fearless diplomat, able to cross over planes of existence with panache, and this ability is a strong symbol for what Shawl suggests is a woman's power: to cross boundaries and make connections in a way that men typically cannot. She's also a model businesswoman, and the story shows the threats that men feel in reaction to her, as much as the power she has over them. Fulla Fulla matches wits with the King of Ku, but ultimately is forced to stay in the realm of death, while her husband—who ruins her final deal with the King of Death by foolishly "mansplaining" things to her—is fated to fetch meat and other goods for the King from the realm of the living if he wishes to survive. When the husband follows Fulla Fulla's advice to throw away "the beads" that enable travel from one realm to another, we learn the irony of his situation: his wife always knew what was best all along, and seeks it even at her own peril.

The charming folktale approach to the story nicely stages a drama of gender. Fulla Fulla is a smart woman who takes care of her family economically and physically, and when her husband acts in response to what threatens his masculinity, it only leads to loss—symbolized by blowing of the whistle that is no longer responded to: the loneliness he feels without her is his only reward, even if patriarchy—embodied by the king who still requests the man's hunting quarry—has spared his life.

—Michael Arnzen, PhD

Otherwise

"LET'S CROSS IT WHILE IT'S STILL FLOATING."

Aim was always in a hurry these days. Nearly eighteen, and she didn't figure she had a whole lot of time left before she'd go Otherwise.

"Hold up," I told her, and she listened. I listened, too, and I heard that weird noise again above the soft wind: an engine running. That was what cars sounded like; they used to fill the roads, back when I was only eleven. Some of the older models still worked—the ones built without no chips.

A steady purr, like a big, fat cat—and there, I saw a glint moving far out on the bridge: sun on a hood or windshield. I raised my binoculars and confirmed it: a pickup truck, headed our way, east, coming toward us out of Seattle.

"What, Lo?" Aim asked.

If I could see them, maybe they could see us. "Come on. Bring the rolly; I'll help." We lifted our rolling suitcase together and I led us into the bushes crowding over the road's edge. Leaves and thorns slashed at our pant legs and sleeves and faces—I beat them away and found a kind of clear area in their middle. Maybe there used to be something, a concrete pad for trash cans or something there. Moss, black and dry from the summer, crunched as we walked over it. We lowered the suitcase, heavy with Aim's tools, and I was about to explain to her why we were hiding but by now that truck was loud and I could tell she heard it, too. All she said was, "What are they gonna think if they see our tracks disappear?"

I had a knife, and I kept it sharp. I pulled it out of the leather sheath I'd made. That was answer enough for Aim. She smiled—a nasty smile, but I loved it the way I loved everything about her: her smell; her long braids; her grimy, stubby nails.

I thought we'd lucked out when the truck barreled by fast—must have been going thirty miles an hour—but then it screeched to a stop. Two doors creaked open. Boot heels clopped on the asphalt. Getting louder. Pausing about even with where I'd ducked us off into the brush.

"Hey!" A dude. "You can come out—we ain't gonna do ya no harm."

Neither one of us moved a hair. Swearing, then thrashing noises, more swearing, louder as Truckdude crashed through the blackberries. He'll never find us, I thought, and I was right. It was his partner who snuck up on our other side, silent as a tick.

"Got 'em, Claude," he yelled, standing up from the weeds with a gun in his hand. He waved it at me and Aim and spoke in a normal tone. "You two can get up if you want. But do it slow."

He raised his voice again. "Chicas. One of 'em's kinda pretty but the other's fat," he told Claude. "You wanna arm wrestle?"

Claude stopped swearing but kept breaking branches and tearing his clothes as he whacked his way over to us. I stayed hunkered down so they'd underestimate me, and so my knife wouldn't fall out from where I had it clamped between my thighs. I felt Aim's arm tremble against mine as Claude emerged from the shadows. She'd be fine, though. Exactly like on a salvage run. I leaned against her a second to let her know that.

The dude with the gun looked a little older than us. Not much older, of course, or he'd have already gone Otherwise, found his own pocket universe, like nearly everyone else whose brain had reached "maturity"—at least that's how the rumors went.

Claude looked my age, or a year or two younger: fourteen, fifteen. He and his partner had the same brown hair and squinty eyes; brothers, then. Probably.

I leered up at Guntoter. "You wanna watch me and her do it first?"

He spat on my upturned face. "Freak! You keep quiet till I tell you talk." The spit tickled as it ran down my cheek.

I didn't hate him. Didn't have the time; I was too busy planning my next move.

"Hey, Dwight, what you think they got in here?" Claude had found our suitcase and given me a name for Guntoter.

"Open 'er up and find out, dickhead."

I couldn't turn around to see the rolly without looking away from Dwight, which didn't seem like a good idea. I heard its zipper and the clink of steel on steel: chisels, hammers, wrenches, clamps, banging against each other as they spilled out on the ground.

"Whoa! Looky at these, Claude. You think that ugly one knows how to use this stuff?" Dwight took his eyes off us and lowered the gun like I'd been waiting for him to do. I launched myself at his legs, a two-hundred-twenty-pound dodgeball. Heard a crack as his left knee bent backward. Then a loud shot from his gun—but only one before I had my knife at his throat.

"*Eennngh!*" he whined. Knee must have hurt, but my blade poking against the underside of his chin kept his mouth shut.

I nodded at Aim and she relieved him of his gun. Claude had run off—I heard him thrashing through the bushes in the direction of the road. "Be right back, Lo." Aim was fine, as I'd predicted, thinking straight and acting cool. She stalked after her prey calm and careful, gun at the ready.

I rocked back on my haunches, easing off Dwight's ribs a bit. That leg had to be fractured. *Problema*; how was I supposed to deal with him, wounded like this? Maybe I shouldn't have hit him so hard. Not as if I could take him to a hospital. I felt him sucking in his breath, winding up for a scream, and sank my full weight on his chest again.

"Lo! You gotta come here!" Aim yelled from the road.

Come there? What? "Why? You can't handle—You didn't let him get his truck back, did—"

"Just come!" She sounded pissed.

Dwight wasn't going anywhere on his own any time soon, but just in case I tugged off his belt and boots and jeans and took away the rest of his weapons: a razor poking through a piece of wood, a folding knife with half the blade of mine, and a long leather bag filled with something heavier than sand. I only hurt him a little stripping off the jeans.

I got to my feet and looked down a second, wondering if I should shoot the man and get his misery over with. Even after years of leading salvage runs I didn't have it in me, though.

I loaded dude's junk and Aim's spilled-out tools in the rolly and dragged it along behind me into the bushes. When he saw I was leaving him he started hollering for help like it might come. That worried me. I hurried out to Aim. Had Claude somehow armed himself?

Claude was nowhere in sight. Aim stood by the truck—our truck, now. She had the door open, staring inside. The gun—our gun, now—hung loose in one hand and the other stretched inside. "Come on," she said, not to me. "It's okay." She hauled her hand back with a kid attached: white with brown hair, like his brothers. They must have been his brothers—I got closer and saw he had that same squintiness going on.

"Look," I said, "leave him here and climb in. If they got any back-up—"

Boom!

Shotguns make a hecka loud noise. Pellets and gravel went pinging off the road. Scared me so much I swung the rolly up into the truck bed by myself. Then I shoved Aim through the door and jumped in after her. Turned the ignition—they had left the key in it—and backed out of there fast as I could rev. Maybe forty feet along, I swung around and switched to second gear. I hit third by the time we made the bridge, jouncing over pits in the asphalt. Some sections were awful low—leaky pontoons. Next storm would sink the whole thing, Aim had said. I told myself if the thing held up on the dudes' ride over here it was gonna be fine for us heading back.

I looked to my right. Aim had pushed the kid ahead of her so he was huddled against the far door. I braked. "Okay, here you go." But he made no move to leave. "What's the matter, you think I'll shoot? Go on, we won't hurt you."

"He's shaking," Aim reported. "Bad. I think he's freaking out."

"Well that's great. Open the door for him yourself then, and let's go."

"No."

I sighed. Aim had this stubbornness no one would suspect unless they spent a long time with her. "Listen, Aim, it was genius to keep him till I drove out of shooting range, but—"

"We can't just dump him off alone."

"He's not alone; his brothers are right behind us!"

"One of 'em with a broken leg."

"Knee." But I took her point. "So, yeah, they're not gonna be much use for making this little guy feel all better again real soon. C'est la flippin vie." I reached past her to the door handle. She looked at me and I dropped my hand in my lap. "Aw, Aim . . . "

Aim missed her family. I knew all about how they'd gone on vacation to Disney World without her when she insisted she was too old for that stuff. Their flights back got canceled, first one, then the next, and the next, till no one pretended anymore there might be another, and the cells stopped working and the last bus into Pasco unloaded and they weren't on it.

"Hector—" She couldn't say more than his name.

"Aim, he's twelve now. He's fine. Even if your—" Even if her mom and dad had deserted him like so many other parents, leaving our world to live Otherwise, where they had anything, everything, whatever they wanted, same as when they drank the drug, but now for always. Or so the rumors said. Perfect homes. Perfect jobs. Perfect daughters. Perfect sons.

"All right. Kid, you wanna come with us or stay here with—um, Claude and Dwight?"

Nothing.

I tried again. "Kid, we gotta leave. We're meeting a friend in—" In the rearview I saw five dudes on foot racing up the road. One waved a long, thin black thing over his head. That shotgun? I slammed the truck out of neutral and tore off. They dwindled in the dust.

Aim punched my shoulder and grinned at me. "You done good," she said. I looked and she had one arm around the little kid, holding him steady, so I concentrated on finding a path for the truck that included mostly even pavement.

Here came the tunnel under Mercer Island. Scary, and not only because its lights were bound to be out—I turned the trucks' on and they made bright spots on the ivy hanging over the tunnel's mouth. That took care of that. Better than if we'd been on foot, even.

But richies... more of them had stayed around than went Otherwise. Which made sense; they had their own drugs they used instead of Likewise, and everything already perfect anyway. Or everything used to be perfect for them till too many ordinary people left and they couldn't find no one to scrub their toilets or take out their garbage. Only us.

When things got bad and the governments broke down, richies were the law, all the law around. What they wanted they got, in this world as much as any Otherwise. And what they wanted was slaves. Servants, they called us, but slaves is what it really was; who'd want to spend whatever time they had before they went Otherwise on doing stupid jobs for somebody else? Nobody who wasn't forced to.

We drove through the ivy curtain. I jabbed on the high beams and slowed to watch for nets or other signs of ambush. Which of course there were gonna be none, because hadn't this very truck come through here less than half an hour ago? But.

"Can't be too careful." Aim always knew what I was thinking.

The headlights caught on a heap of something brown and gray spread over most of the road and I had two sets of choices: speed up, or slow down more; drive right over it, or swerve around. I picked A and A: stomped the gas pedal and held the steering wheel tight. Suddenly closer I saw legs, arms, bloated faces, smelled the stink of death. I felt the awful give beneath our tires. It was a roadblock of bodies—broken glass glittered where we would have gone if I'd tried to avoid them, and two fresh corpses splayed on the concrete, blood still wet and red. A trap, but a sprung one. Thanks, Claude. Thanks, Dwight.

The pile of rotting dead people fell behind us mercifully fast. I risked a glance at the kid. He stared straight forward like we were bringing him home from seeing a movie he had put on mental replay. Like there was nothing to see outside the truck and never had been and never would be.

"Maybe this was what freaked him out in the first place?" asked Aim. "You know, before he even got to us?" It was a theory.

We came out into the glorious light again. One more short tunnel as the road entered the city was how I remembered the route. I stopped the truck to think. When my fingers started aching I let go of the wheel.

A bird landed on a loose section of the other bridge that used to run parallel. Fall before last it had been the widest of its kind in the world, according to Aim.

She cared about those kinds of things.

The sun was fairly high yet. We'd left our camp in the mountains early this morning and come twelve mostly downhill miles before meeting up with the kid's brothers. The plan had been to cross the bridge inconspicuously, on foot, hole up in Seward Park with the Rattlers and wait for Rob to show. Well, we'd blown the inconspicuous part.

"Sure you don't wanna go back?" I asked Aim. "They'll be glad to see us. And the truck'll make it a short trip, and it's awesome salvage, too . . . "I trailed off.

"You can if you rather." But she knew the answer. I didn't have to say it. Aim was why I'd stayed in Pasco instead of claiming a place on the res, which even a mix had a right to do. Now I had come with her this far for love. And I'd go further. To the edge of the continent. All the way.

Rob had better be worth it, though. With his red hair and freckles and singing and guitar-playing Aim couldn't shut up about since we got his message. And that secret fire she said was burning inside him like a cigarette, back when they were at their arts camp. He better be worthy of *her*.

"Stop pouting." She puckered her face and crossed her eyes. "Your face will get stuck like that. Let me drive. Chevies are sweet." She handed me the gun, our only distance weapon—and I hadn't even gotten Dwight's cartridges, but too late to think of that—then slid so her warm hip pressed against mine for a moment. "Go on. Get out."

The kid didn't move when I opened the passenger door so I crawled in over him.

Aim drove like there was traffic: careful, using signals. Guess she learned it from watching her folks. The tunnel turned out clear except for a couple of crappy modern RVs no one had bothered torching yet. One still had curtains in its smashed windows, fluttering when we went by. We exited onto the main drag—Rainier Avenue, I recalled. Aim braked at the end of the ramp. "Which way?"

"South." I pointed left.

Rainier had seen some action. Weed-covered concrete rubble

lined the road's edges, narrowing it to one lane. A half-burned restaurant sign advertised hotcakes. A sandbag bunker, evidently empty, guarded an intersection filled with a downed walkway. A shred of tattered camo clung to a wrecked lamppost. Must be relics of the early days; soldiers had been some of the first outside jail to head Otherwise, deserting in larger and larger numbers as real life got lousier and lousier.

"Wow. What a mess." Aim eased over a spill of bricks and stayed in low gear to rubberneck. "How're we gonna get off of this and find the park?"

"Uhhh." Would we have to dig ourselves a turnoff? No— "Here!" More sandbags, but some had tumbled down from their makeshift walls, and we only had to shove a few aside to reach a four-lane street straight to the lakeshore. We followed that around to where the first of the Rattlers' lookouts towered up like a giant birdhouse for ostriches with fifty-foot legs. A chica had already sighted us and trained her slingshot on the truck's windshield. Her companion called out and we identified ourselves enough that they let us through to the gate in their chain-link fence. Another building, this one more like the bunker on Rainier, blocked the way inside. Four Rattlers were stationed here, looking like paintball geeks gone to heaven. We satisfied them of our bona fides, too, using the sheet of crypto and half a rubber snake their runner had turned over with Rob's message. They took my knife. I didn't blame 'em. They let us keep our gun, but minus the bullets.

"What's in the back?"

I hadn't even looked after tossing up the rolly. Dumb. When the sentries opened the big metal drums, though, they found nothing but fuel in them, no one hiding till they could bust out and slit our throats.

Four of those, and the rest of the bed was filled with covered five-gallon tubs: white plastic, the high grade kind you use to ferment beer in. And that's what was in the ten they checked.

"Welcome home," one chica maybe my age said. Grudgingly, but she said it. She walked ahead to guide us into their main camp.

Didn't take her long. A few minutes and I saw fire pits, and picnic tables set together in parts of circles, tarps strung between trees over platforms, a handful of big tents. We pulled up next to their playground as the sun was barely beginning to wonder was it time to set. The chica banged on our hood twice, then nodded and scowled at us. Aim nodded too and shut off the ignition.

The kid opened the truck's passenger door. Aim and I looked at each other in silence. Then she grinned. "I guess we're there yet!"

Maybe it was the other littles on the swings and jungle gyms that got through to him. He slid to the ground and walked a few steps toward them, then stopped. I got out too and slammed the door. Didn't faze him. He was focused on the fun and games.

"What have we here?" A longhaired dude wearing a mustache and a skirt came over from watching the littles play.

Aim opened her door and got out too. "We're a day or so early I guess—Amy Niehauser and Dolores Grant." I always tease Aim about how she ended up with such a non-Hispanic name, and she gives me grief right back about not having something made-up, like "Shaniqua" or "Running Fawn." "We're from Kiona. In Pasco?"

Dude nodded. "Sure. Since Britney was bringing you in I figured that was who you must be. I'm Curtis. We weren't expecting a vehicle, though." He waved a hand at the truck.

Britney had hopped up on the bed again while we talked, lifting the lids off the rest of the plastic tubs. "Likewise!" she shouted. "Look at this!"

Aim and I leaned up over the side to see. Britney was tearing off cover after cover. Sure enough, the five tubs furthest in were all at least three-quarters full of thick, indigo blue liquid with specks of pale purple foam. I had never seen so much Likewise in one place.

Curtis lost his cool. "What the hell! We told you we don't allow that—that—" He didn't have the vocabulary to call the drug a bad enough name.

"No, it's not ours—we stole this truck and we didn't know—" Aim tried to calm him down. She tugged at the tub nearest the end. "Here, we'll help you pour 'em in the lake."

"You seriously think we wanna pollute our water like that?"

"Look, I'm just saying we'll get rid of it. We didn't know, we just took this truck from some dudes acting like cowboys on the other side of the bridge, the little dude's big brothers, and they had a few friends—"

That got Britney's attention. "They follow you?"

"Not real far," I said, breaking in. "Since when we took this we left 'em on foot." And they hadn't shot at us more than once—the fuel explained why. "They ain't the only trouble you got for neighbors, either—I'd be more worried about Mercer Island if I were you than them bridge dudes—or a load of Likewise we can dump anywhere you want."

"Right." Curtis seemed to quiet down and consider this. "Yeah, we'll dig a hole or something . . . "

No one had proved a connection between Likewise and all the adults talking about living Otherwise, then disappearing. No one had proved anything in a long time that I'd heard of. But the prisons where it first got made were the same ones so many "escaped" from early on, which is the only reason anyone even noticed a bunch of poor people had gone missing, IMO. News reports began about the time it was getting so popular outside, here and in a few more countries.

Some of us still cooked it up. Some of us still drank it. How long did the side-effects last? If you indulged at the age of sixteen would you vanish years later, as soon as your brain was ready? Could you even tell whether you went or not?

The ones who knew were in no position to tell us. They were Otherwise.

Britney went to report us to the committee, she said. A pair of twelve-year-olds came and showed us where to unload the fuel drums. I helped Aim lower the rolly from the bed—how had I got it up there on my own? My arms were gonna hurt bad when the adrenaline wore off—and she handed them the keys. They drove to the bunker with the Likewise for the sentries to watch over.

Aim had to head back to the playground after that. The little dude seemed thoroughly recovered: he'd thrown off his jacket and was running wild and yelling with the other kids like he belonged there.

The Rattlers' committee met with us over dinner in this ridiculous tipi they'd rigged up down by the swimming beach. Buffaloes and lightning painted on the sides. I mean, even I knew tipis were plains technology and had nothing to do with tribes in these parts. But, well, the Rattlers acted proud and solemn bringing us inside, telling us to take off our shoes and which way to circle around the fire, and damn if they didn't actually pass a real, live pipe after feeding us salads plus some beige glop that looked a lot worse than it tasted. And tortillas, which they insisted on calling fry bread.

Tina, their eldest, sat on a sofa cushion; she looked maybe Aim's age, but probably she was older. Trying to show the rest of the committee how to run things when she was gone Otherwise, she asked about folks at Kiona: who had hooked up with who, how many pregnant, any cool salvage we'd come across, any adults we'd noticed still sticking around. Aim answered her.

There were two dudes, one on either side of Tina—husbands, maybe?—Rattlers were known for doing that kinda thing—and a couple younger chicas chiming in with compliments about how well we were doing for ourselves. I waited politely for them to raise the subject they wanted to talk about. Which was, as I'd figured, the five tubs of Likewise.

They decided to forgive us and opted to pour 'em in a hole like Aim suggested.

Tina had brains. "What's interesting is that they were bringing this shipment *out* of Seattle." She stretched her legs straight, pointed her toes up and pushed toward the fire with her wool-socked heels. August, and the evenings were on the verge of chilly.

"Not like the whole city's sworn off," one of the chicas ventured to say.

"Yeah." I had the dude that agreed pegged for a husband because he wore a ring matching the one on Tina's left hand. "That crew up in Gas Works? They could be brewing big old vats of Likewise and how would we know?"

The second dude chimed in. "They sure wouldn't expect us to barter for any." He wore a ring that matched the one on Tina's right.

The young chica who'd already spoken wondered if it was their responsibility to keep the whole of Seattle clean, suburbs too. Husband One opined that they'd better think a while about that.

"Next question." That was Tina again. "What are those bridge boys gonna do to get their shipment back?" She looked at me, though it was Aim who started talking.

We hadn't told Claude or Dwight where we were going, or made a map for 'em or anything, so I thought the Rattlers were pretty safe. Plus I had hurt Dwight, broken at least one bone. But the committee decided the truck was a liability even if they painted it, and told us we better take it with us when we departed their territory. Which would have to be soon—"Tomorrow?" asked Husband Two.

Aim folded her lips between her front teeth a few seconds in that worried way she had. We'd expected more of a welcome, considering her skills. Kinda hoped she'd be able to set up a forge here for at least a week. Were the Rattlers gonna make us miss her date with Rob? But according to the committee's spies he was close, already landed on this side of the Sound and heading south. He'd arrive any minute now. So we could keep our rendezvous.

Dammit.

Then I finally got to find out more on where all those corpses in the tunnel came from: richies, as I'd suspected. Didn't seem like the committee wanted to go further into it, though. The dead people were who? People the richies had killed. How? Didn't know. Didn't think it mattered; dead was dead. And why were they stacked up on the road all unhygienic-like instead of properly buried? Have to send a detail to take care of that. And the two fresh ones? Tina said she figured the way I did that they were fallout from Claude and Dwayne's trip through the blockade.

So why? Well, that was obvious, too: use the dead ones to catch us, alive, to work for 'em.

It became more obvious when Curtis took us to where we were supposed to sleep: a tree house far up the central hill of the park's peninsula. He climbed the rope ladder ahead of us and showed us the pisspot, the water bucket and dipper, the bell to ring if one of us suddenly took violently ill in the night. Then he wanted to know if we'd seen his little sister's body in the pile.

"Uh, no, we kinda—we had to go fast, didn't see much. Really." Aim could tell a great lie.

"She had nice hair, in ponytails. And big, light green eyes."

Anybody's eyes that had been open in that pile, they weren't a color you'd recognize anymore. Mostly they were gone. Along with big chunks of face. "No, we, uh, we had to get out of there too fast. Really didn't see. Sorry."

He left us alone at last.

Alone as we were going to get—there was a lot of other tree

houses nearby; dusk was settling in fast but we could see people moving up their own ladders, hear 'em talking soft and quiet.

"Lie down." I patted the floor mat. She came into my arms. I had her body, no problema. I did hurt from heaving the rolly around, but that didn't matter much. I stroked her bangs back from her pretty face that I knew even in the dark.

"What'd they do with Dwayne?"

"Who?"

"Dwayne, you know, the little dude?"

Right: Claude and Dwight's kid brother. "That what you wanna call him?"

Aim snorted. "It's his *name*. He told Curtis. I heard him."

My fingers wandered down to the arches of her eyebrows, smoothing them flat. "You worried about him? He looked happy on the playground. They must have places for kids to sleep here. We seen plenty of 'em."

"Yeah. You're right." The skin above her nose crinkled. I traced her profile, trying to give her something else to think of. It sort of worked.

"Why don't the committee care more about the Mercer Island richies? That was—horrible. In the tunnel."

I laughed, though it wasn't the littlest bit funny. "Fail. Mega Fail—they were supposed to be protecting these people here and the richies raided 'em. I wouldn't wanna talk about it either."

I felt her forehead relax. "Yeah." She reached up and tugged my scarf free so she could run her hands over my close-clipped scalp. That was more like it. I snuggled my head against the denim of her coat.

That was our last night together as a couple.

She only mentioned Rob once.

Next morning my arm felt even sorer. And my shoulder had turned stiff. And my wrist. Was getting old like this? No wonder people went Otherwise.

Aim and I woke up at the same time, same as at home and on salvage runs. "Good dreams?" I asked. She nodded and gave me a sheepish half-smile, so I didn't have to ask who she'd dreamed about. It wasn't me.

What kind of universe would Aim make if she went Otherwise? It wouldn't be the same as mine.

Curtis had pointed out a latrine on the way to our treehouse. We dumped the pisspot there and took care of our other morning needs. It was a nice latrine, with soap and a bowl of water.

Down we went, following the trail to the main camp. Aim held my hand when we could walk side by side. Sweet moments. I knew I better treasure 'em.

I helped set out breakfast, which was berries and bars of what appeared to be last night's beige glop, fossilized. Aim retrieved the rolly from where we'd left it under a supply tarp. She cleaned the gun, which she called Walter, and shined up her tools. Soon enough she attracted a clientele.

First come a dude could have been fourteen or fifteen; he wanted her to help him fix up an underwater trap for turtles and crayfish. Then he had a friend a little older who asked her to help him take apart a motor to power his boat. Actually, he had taken it apart already, and wanted her to put it together again with him.

Aim called a break for herself after a couple hours of this so she could go check out how Dwayne was doing. And she wanted to bring him a plum from the ones I collected for snacks. I waited by the tools for her to come back. A shadow cut the warm sun and I looked up from the dropcloth.

"Hey." A dude's voice. All I could see was a silhouette. Like an eclipse—a gold rim around darkness.

"Hey back."

"You're not Amy."

"Nope."

He sat down fast, folding his legs. "Must be Dolores, then? I'm Rob." He held out a hand to shake, so I took it.

Now I could see him, dude was every bit as pretty as Aim had said. Dammit. Hair like new copper, tied back smooth and bright and loose below a wide-brimmed straw fedora. Eyes large, a strange, pale blue. Freckles like cinnamon all over his snub-nosed face and his long arms where they poked out of the black-and-white print shirt he wore. But not on his throat, which was smooth as vanilla ice cream and made me want to—no. This was Aim's crush.

His hand was a little damp around the palm. Fingers long and strong. I let it go. "Aim's around here somewhere; she'll be back in a minute, I think, if you wanna wait."

"Sure." He had a tiny little stick, a twig, in the corner of his mouth. His lips were pink, not real thin for a white boy. Dammit.

"Where's your guitar?" I asked.

"Left it back home, at the bunkers. The Herons'll take care of it for me; too much to travel with. But I packed my pennywhistle." He swapped the stick for something longer, shiny black and silver. He played a sad-sounding song, mostly slow, with some fast parts where one line ended and the next began. Then he speeded up, did a new, sort of jazzy tune. Then another, and I recognized it: "Firework."

Aim recognized it, too. Or him, anyway—she came running up behind me shouting his name: "Rob! Rob!" She hauled him up with a hug. "I'm so glad! So glad!" He hugged her back. They both laughed and leaned away enough to look each other in the eyes.

"Oh, wow—" "Did you—" They started and stopped talking at the same time. Cute.

Dwayne had showed up in Aim's wake. He stood to one side, hands in his front pockets, about as awkward as I felt.

Rob and Aim let go of each others' arms. "Who's this?" he asked her, bending his knees to put his face on the kid's level.

"I'm Dwayne. I come all the way from Issaquah." Which was nine times more words than I'd ever heard him use before. Maybe he liked white dudes.

"That's pretty far. But I met somebody came even further."

"Who're you?"

"I'm Rob. I live in Fort Worden, other side of the Sound."

"Issaquah is twenty-two miles from Seattle."

"Well, this chica I'm talking about sailed to Fort Worden over the ocean from Liloan. That's in the Philippines. Six thousand miles."

"She did not!"

"I'm telling you."

Here came Curtis over from the playground. He said hey and dragged Dwayne back with him with the promise of a swim, "—so you can get packed quick."

The Rattlers wanted us gone yesterday. While Rob met with their committee to tell them the news out of Liloan—how the Philippines had been mostly missed by the EMPs and other tech-killers thrown around in the first mass panic—Aim loaded her tools in the rolly, and I went to find the truck. At the fuel shed they directed me up the remains of a service road. The twelve-year-olds had parked at the end of it; they were just through filling in the hole they'd dug, tamping down dirt with a couple of shovels. The empty Likewise tubs lay on their sides in the dead pine needles.

"Thanks," I said. "We were gonna do that."

"'S'all right," the bigger one said. "Didn't take long."

"Yes, it did." Her friend wasn't about to lie. "But we're done, now, and nobody drunk it.

"Have you ever—" The smaller girl smacked the bigger one on her head. "Stop! I was only asking!" She turned to me again. "You ever taken any Likewise yourself?"

Once. A single dose was low risk—I'd heard of adults with the same history as me, twenty-four, twenty-five, and still not Otherwise.

"Tastes like dog slobber," I told her. "Like spit bugs crapped in a bottle of glue."

"Eeuuw!" They made faces and giggled. I thought about the questions they didn't ask as they brought me back down in the truck. About how Likewise felt, what happened when I had it in me.

You could call it a dream. In it, my mom had never hit me and my dad had never got stoned. I was living in a house with Aim. The drug was specific: a yellow house with white trim, a picket fence. We had a dog named Quincy Jones and a parakeet named Sam. The governments were still running everything. We had a kid and jobs we went to. I remember falling asleep and waking up and getting maybe a little bored at work, but basically being happy. So happy.

Seemed like it went on for years. I was out for eight hours.

We could have driven all the way to Fort Worden, only Aim wanted to see the Space Needle. "C'mon, when are we gonna have another chance?"

I rolled my eyes. "You can *see* it from freakin' *anywhere*, Aim. Ask *them* if *they* see it." I pointed up at the chicas in the fifty-foot-high lookout.

"Okay. Touch it then. I mean touch it."

Our first fight.

Of course Rob took her side. "Yeah, the truck; tough to let it go, but there's no connections for us in Tacoma. Olympia either; can't say who or what we might run into going south. I told the captain up at Edmonds I'd be back in a week. Maybe he can stow it for us? And even if we're early that's our best bet. North. So the Space Needle's not much of a detour."

Aim looked at me. "*All flippin' right,*" I said.

I drove again. Aim took the middle seat, but it wasn't me she pressed up against.

Rattlers had told us where to avoid, and I did my best. From Rainier I had to guess the route, and sometimes I guessed wrong. And sometimes my guesses would have been good if the roads didn't have huge holes in 'em or obstacles too hard to move out of our way. We didn't see anyone else, only signs they'd been around: coiled up wires, stacks of wood—not a surprise, since anyone on a scavenge run would have lookouts. Groups had mainly settled in parks where you could grow crops, and we weren't trying to cross those.

We reached Seattle Center late. No time to find anywhere else to spend the night.

There'd been action here, too. I remembered the news stories, though they hadn't made any sense. Not then, and not now—why would anyone fight over such a place, so far off from any water? But tanks had crawled their way onto the grounds, smashing trees and sculptures, shooting fire and smoke back and forth. They left scars we could still see: burned-out buildings, craters, bullet holes.

The Space Needle stood in the middle of about an acre of blackberries covering torn-up concrete—what used to be a plaza. Old black soot and orange rust marked its once-white legs. I tooled us under a pair of concrete pillars for the dead Monorail and backed in as close as I could get without slicing open a tire. "There you go," I said. "Touch it." Which was a little mean, I admit.

Rob climbed out the window without opening the door and got up on the truck cab's roof. He stuck his arm in and hauled Aim after him. I heard the two of 'em talking about chopping a path through the thorns if they'd had swords, and how to forge them, and a trick Aim knew called damascening. Aim recited her facts about how high the thing was, how long it took to erect, et cetera.

Then I didn't hear anything for a while. Then her breath. I turned on the radio, like there'd be something more than static to cover up the sounds they were going to make.

One of them shifted and the metal above my head popped in and out. That gave me courage to hit the horn—a short blast like it was an accident—and open the door. Very, very slowly.

Shin deep in brambles I unhooked from my pants one by one, I took a blanket from the boxes of supplies the Rattlers sent us off with. Then I couldn't help myself; I looked. They both had all their clothes on and were sitting up. For the moment. Aim waved. Rob pretended to stroke a beard he didn't have and smiled.

"In a minute," I said, meaning I'd come back. Eventually. Give me strength, I thought, and I smiled, too, and waded carefully along the trail the truck had smashed.

She wanted to be with him. I loved her anyhow. To the edge of the continent. All the way.

I would follow her.

But tonight I would sleep alone.

At least that was the plan. When it came down to it, though, I didn't dare rest my eyes. Dark was falling. The place was too open—bad juju. I had a feeling, once I got out from under my jealousy. So I found a trash barrel, rolled it up a ramp in the side of some place looked like a giant scorched wad of metal gum. I set the barrel upright, climbed and balanced on its rim, and scrabbled from there to lie on my stomach on a low roof—must have been the only flat surface to the whole building, even before the howitzers and grenade-launchers and whatever else attacked it.

Me and Walter settled in to keep watch. The Rattlers had returned his magazine when they gave me back my knife, and there were seven rounds left.

Aim and Rob were maybe fifty feet south. I still heard 'em clear enough to keep me awake till Claude and his friends showed up.

Trying to be smart, the bridge dudes turned off whatever vehicle they drove blocks away. The engine's noise was a clue, and its silence was another. Insects went quiet to my east in case I needed a third.

Starlight's not the best to see by. I couldn't really count 'em—four or five dudes it must be, I figured, same as yesterday. They zeroed in on Aim and Rob, who were talking again.

"Hands up!" a dude commanded. How were they gonna tell, I wondered, but one of 'em opened the truck door and the courtesy light came on. There was Aim and Rob, a bit tousled up. Too bad I didn't want to shoot *them*. Couldn't get a line on anyone else.

"Get your sorry asses outta me and Dwight's—outta my truck." That would be Claude.

"Daddy? Where's Daddy?" And that would be that kid Dwayne? His age was all wrong for Dwight to be his dad, but who else was it rising out of that supply box, pale-faced in the yellow courtesy light?

The kid must have stowed away. He held out his arms and kicked free of something and Claude stepped up to grab and lift him and now I had a great shot. Couldn't have been better. But I didn't take it.

Next minute I wished I had when dudes on either side yanked Aim and Rob out of opposite doors. I heard her yell at them and get slapped.

Someone else was yelling, too—not me, I was busy shimmying off the roof while there was cover for my noise. "No! Don't hit her! No! Put me down!" Little Dwayne was on our side?

Brightness. Someone had switched on the truck's headlamps. I ducked down. Aim was crying hard. They shoved her to the pavement. I hadn't heard a peep outta Rob. When they marched him into the light I saw one dude's hand over his mouth and a shiny piece of metal right below his ear. Knife or a gun—didn't matter which. Woulda kept me quiet, too.

Only four of 'em. Plus Dwayne. Seven bullets seemed plenty—if I didn't mind losing Rob.

I didn't. But Aim would.

Bang! Bang! Walter wasn't quite loud as a shotgun. Glass and metal pinged off the pavement, flew away into the sudden dark. Only one round each for the truck's headlamps. I was proud of myself.

Light still came out of the cab from the overhead courtesy. Not much. I couldn't see anybody.

But I could hear 'em shouting to each other to find the chica, and shooting. Randomly, I hoped. No screams, so Rob had probably got away all right.

I shifted position, which made the next part trickier, but would keep the dudes guessing where to kill me. I went round to one side, with the frame of the open driver's door blocking my vision. Walter stayed steady—I gripped him with both hands and squeezed. Got it in one. I was good. Total night, now. I squirmed off on my belly for a ways to be sure no one had a flashlight, then crawled, then stumbled to my feet and walked. Headed north by the stars, with nothing on me but Walter, my knife, my binoculars. A blanket. Not even a bottle for water.

It was a shame to leave all the provisions the Rattlers had given us. And too bad I had to damage a high-functioning machine like that truck. Aim would cuss me out for it when we caught up with one another at Edmonds.

Aim would be fine. She always was. Rob, too, most likely.

I took the rest of that night and part of a day to walk there. It was easy: 99 most of the way. The stars were enough to see that by, and the Aurora Bridge was practically intact. I wondered what facts Aim would have told me about it if we were going over it together. All I knew was people used to kill themselves here by jumping off. Kids? Didn't we used to have the highest rates of suicide?

If Aim didn't show up at Edmonds in a few days maybe I'd come back. Or find some Likewise.

I snuck in the dark past where they used to have a zoo, worried I might run into some weird predator. I didn't; when the animals got out they must've headed for the lake on the road's other side.

The sky got lighter and I began to look for pursuit as well as listening for it. Nobody came. The stores and restaurants lining the highway would have been scavenged out long ago. I was alone.

No Aim in sight.

Rain started to fall. I hung the blanket over my head like the Virgin Mary. Because of the clouds it was hard to tell time, but I figured I turned onto 104 a couple of hours after sunrise.

I went down a long slope to the water. Rob had said if we got split up to meet by a statue of sea lions on the beach.

This was my first time to be at the ocean. It was big, but I could see land out in its middle. Looked like I could just swim there.

Route 104 continued right on into the water. The statue was supposed to be to its south. The sand moved, soft and tiresome under my wet chucks. I spotted a clump of kids digging for something further toward the water, five or six of 'em. They didn't try to stop me and I kept on without asking directions. A couple of 'em had slings out, but I must not have seemed too threatening; neither chica pointed 'em my way.

A metal seal humped up some stairs to a patch of green. Was this the place? I climbed up beside it. At the top, a garden. I could tell it was a garden since it wasn't blackberries, though I had no idea what these plants were. But they grew in circles and lines, real patterns. And more metal seal sculptures—okay, sea lions—stuck out from between them.

Definitely. I was here. I curled up in the statue's shelter and the rain stopped. I fell asleep.

A whisper woke me. "Lo!" My heart revved. Aim? Eyes open, all I saw was Rob.

"You can't call me that."

"Sorry. Didn't want you to shoot me."

I sat up straight and realized I had Walter in my hand. Falling asleep hadn't been so stupid after all.

Rob's ice cream throat had a red inch-long slice on one side, so it had been a knife the bridge dude held there. He seemed fine besides that. "Is she around?" he asked. "She and you came together?" I shook my head and he folded up his legs and sat down beside me. Too close. I scooted over.

We didn't say anything for a long time. Could have been an hour. I was thirsty. And hungry. I wondered if maybe I ought to eat from the garden.

Rob held out his water bottle for me and I took it and drank. When I gave it back he didn't even wipe the mouth off.

The clouds pulled themselves apart and let this beautiful golden orange light streak through. The sun was going down. I'd slept the whole afternoon.

"Look," said Rob. "Look. I know you and Aim—"

"You can't call her that."

"Yes I can! Listen. Look. You were with her before me and I don't want to—to mess with that."

As if he hadn't. "And?"

"And—and we were talking." Among other things. "And she

was saying if we got married—if she got married she would want to marry *both* of us."

I stared at him hard to make sure he was serious. Me and Aim had teased each other about being married ever since we met in gym class. Even before people over twenty began going Otherwise.

Apparently I wasn't the only one it was more than a joke for.

"So would you?"

"Would I what?" But I knew.

"Would you freakin marry me! Would you—"

"But I'm a lesbian! You're a dude!"

"Well, duh."

"And only because you wanna hook up with *my* chica? Unh-unh."

"Well, it's not only that."

"Really?" I stood up. He did too. "What, you're in love with me? I'm fat, I'm a big mouth, a smartass—"

"You're plain old smart! And brave, and Aim thinks you're the closest thing to a goddess who ever walked the earth."

"What if I am?" I wanted to leave. But this was where she would come. I had to be here. I wrapped the blanket around me and tucked my arms tight.

"Yeah. What if you are? What if she's right? I kinda think—" He quit talking a minute and looked over his shoulder at the beach. "I kinda think she is. You are."

If he had tried to touch me then I would have knocked the fool unconscious.

Instead, he turned around and looked at the beach again. "That's him," he said. "Captain Lee." He pointed and I saw a bright yellow triangle sailing toward us out of the west. "Our ride's here ahead of time. I have to go meet him and tell him we need to wait for Aim." He left me alone with my wet blanket.

It was almost dark by the time he came back, carrying a bucket. "Here you go. Supper." I was ready to eat, no doubt. Inside was a hot baked yam and some greens with greasy pink fish mixed in. I washed it all down with more of Rob's water.

We took turns hanging out at the statue. Rob had connections with the locals, the Hammerheads and this other group, the Twisters. He stayed with them, and I bunked on Lee's boat.

Three days dragged past. I got used to a certain idea. I let him put his arm around me once when we met on the stairs. And another time when he introduced me to a dude he brought to pick some herbs in the garden—they were for medicines, not that nice to eat.

And another time. We were there together, but with my binoculars I saw her first. I shouted and he hugged me. Both arms. I broke away and ran and ran and yes, it was Aim! And Dwayne, which explained a lot when I thought about it afterward, but I didn't care right then.

"Aim! Aim!" I lifted her in the air and whirled us around and we kissed each other long and hard. I was with her and it was this reality, hers and mine and everybody else's, not one I created just for me. I cried and laughed and yelled at the blue sky, so glad. Oh so freakin' glad.

Of course I had known all along she'd make it.

And then Rob caught up with me and he kissed her too. She held my hand the whole time. So how could I feel jealous and left out?

Well, I could. But that might change, someday. Someday, it might be otherwise.

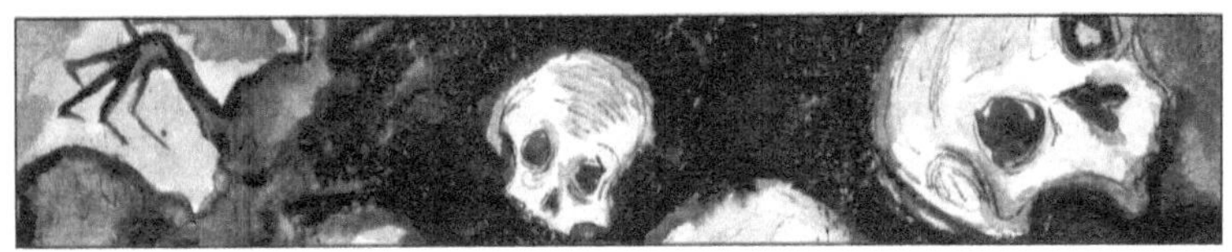

Otherwise: A Commentary

"OTHERWISE" IS AN AMAZING POST-APOCALYPTIC narrative, and feels reminiscent of James Dickey's *Deliverance*, Cormac McCarthy's *The Road*, and PD James's *Children of Men* . . . if they featured young mixed-race women of mixed sexual identification as their lead characters. It's a story that makes you root for these innocent victims trying to survive in a world where the darker side of man—particularly the id-driven laddies of patriarchy—are set free.

Shawl's clever worldview here and the invention of a drug culture that leads to population abandonment (as people choose the drug over life)—is an interesting backdrop for a Huxlean critique of contemporary culture. She describes the essential breakdown of American society as essentially a kind of consumerist addiction and the story critiques culture predominantly along class lines—showing what happens when a gap erupts between servant and elite as the majority of the population "deserts," leaving niche groups of drug dealers and others in nomadic camps for survival. What this social allegory ends up doing, however, is coming back time and again to the issue of love, suggesting that the desire for bonding with the Other is the only hope for mankind. The villains in this tale can be read as embodying that which is an enemy to love, and the unique relationship suggested at the end of the story offers an alternate structure by which love just might be possible in such a world. Somehow, in this apocalyptic look at a dystopian world, a utopian hope for multicultural unity arises. The message? Don't give up.

—Michael Arnzen, PhD

Just Between Us

DOLORES OPENED THE CLOSET DOOR. HERE WAS the problem. A dead woman hung by her neck, suspended from the cross bar by a man's tie. Violet in color, probably silk from the look of the knot. She shut the door quickly and called up her landlady.

Mrs. Pawkes was dressed for golf. Her clothing glowed a golden green in Dolores' vision. Her sharp-chinned, line-seamed face managed to project warm but distracted concern as she assured Dolores that the dead women were nothing to worry about.

"Women? You mean this isn't the only one?"

"Well, I've had to take care of one a week now for—seems like maybe the last couple of months. But it's just like the refugees, isn't it?"

"No, Mrs. Pawkes, it is not." The last time she came in, Dolores had opened the closet door to find a huddled group of thin, brown, anxious people, clutching fearfully at blankets, newspapers, cooking pots. The detritus of displacement. "Corpses smell. Worse," she amended. "And I had to come back before I wanted to. I think they scared Little Girl. She's gone out."

"Oh, I'm so sorry. The poor thing." The image of Mrs. Pawkes switched from head-and-shoulders to full length as she removed her bag of clubs and leaned it against something—a wall or a doorway, it wasn't quite clear. "I wish I'd known. She didn't say anything..."

"Well, what did you expect?" Little Girl was barely verbal. She knew Mrs. Pawkes existed, but there was very little contact between the two.

"I just didn't have anywhere else to put them, Dolores. They keep—popping up. I wish I could tell you where from."

"I'll look into it. Meanwhile, what am I supposed to do about Little Girl?"

"Send someone after her, I guess... unless you'd rather go yourself?"

"You know there isn't room enough for both of us out there."

"Well, I'm sure you'll think of something, dear. You're so resourceful." Mrs. Pawkes glanced longingly over her shoulder at her golf clubs. The vision began to fade. Dolores could have held it together, but what would be the point? As usual, everything was up to her.

She opened her eyes, which she had squeezed shut during the conversation, massaging the wrinkles where her eyebrows furrowed together. She looked around the place. Not bad, except for the smell. She was in the upper story of a white-painted frame house. Old. Interesting. Lots of windows with tiny panes shaped like diamonds, crescents, tears. Hardwood floors, oriental rugs. Little Girl had left her playthings strewn around the apartment: a rocking horse, cardboard boxes painted to look like bricks. A pink tutu and a cone-shaped hat, white-spangled chiffon streaming from its peak. On the enamel-topped kitchen table a bubble pipe and a tub full of sudsy water waited next to a bowl of soggy cereal.

How could Mrs. Pawkes have been so insensitive? This was supposed to be a safe place. Not a morgue. And Little Girl wasn't really equipped to handle most of what went on outside. How to get her back?

She sat down to think on a love-seat that hadn't been there when she came in. It was hers. She recognized the blue wool upholstery from her last time in. The longer she stayed, the more the place would bear her mark.

Send someone after her. Sure, but who? Dolores and Little Girl were the main tenants, the oldest and biggest ones. There were others, though. Neighbors. Guests. Dolores struggled to classify those she knew.

Patcheddy. She was like Little Girl, only thin and weak and poor. That big, red, roaring—Dolores had never given that a name. Call it Red. Red was too scary to help with this. And Patcheddy wasn't much good for anything, except to whine. It had to be someone small enough so they could both fit outside, but strong enough to bring Little Girl back in.

There was a tapping at one of the windows. A big black bird with blue and white wings was pecking at the glass. Dolores got up to let it in, then hesitated with the window open only a crack. "Who is it?"

It was Hermie.

"Oh, yes." Little Girl's imaginary playmate. She swung the casement wide and he flew in. Hermie had come to Little Girl along with the mumps and an interminable stay in bed. Usually, though, he looked more like light reflecting from a glass of water—or nothing at all. "What brings you here? And why so—so—"

So *visible*. The bird cocked his head knowingly. He was practicing. He wanted to go outside, to find Little Girl, and he needed to practice pretending to be real.

"Perfect!" she exclaimed. She sat back down on the love seat, and Hermie hopped onto the far arm. "Thank you, thank you, thank you."

Actually, the going out part would be easy. For him. Finding her, too. But he would need help bringing her back.

"But I'm too big to get outside while she's still there."

But she could help inside. She had to. She had to get rid of the dead women. She had to stop them coming. Otherwise he could find Little Girl, but what good would that do? She'd never come back in.

"Okay, Hermie. Okay. I'll see what I can do." He flew back to the windows. They were French, now, with crystal doorknobs. He flapped back and forth noisily while she walked over, turned a knob and pushed. There was a balcony on the other side, weeping black wrought iron. Hermie flew out over it and became one with the powder blue mist beyond.

Am I all right they keep asking, asking. I always tell them no. My favorite word. It's the best. Nononononono. I use it all the time.

I'm hungry. I want a candy bar, or an ice cream. I ask the waiter for one I remember that is orange. A Dreamsicle is the name. But when it comes it is all melted in a glass. No stick. And it tastes like medicine. Nasty. I drink it anyway.

I try again. A Heath Bar, too, is all melted. Everything in this place is nasty and served in a cup. I'm going to leave. It's closing anyway. They want to know if I need them to call me a cab. I use my word and go.

It's pretty out in the dark. There aren't too many things to see. The wind kisses me with long, dry kisses, brushing down my cheeks. I think the wind is like a pretty young lady aunt. She runs around doing interesting things, so she doesn't have to tell you how big you're getting. And she kisses you, but then she moves away, not holds you tight so you can't go and it's scary and your word won't even work.

There is a park, but I'm not supposed to go in there. Bad men are waiting to hurt a Little Girl. But if they saw me they would think I was big, like Dolores is. Only still they might want to hurt me. Anyway, I don't have to want to go there, because out of the park flies a bird I like. Dark and dry and friendly, the way the wind is in this night. I hold out my finger and he grabs it with his feet. It hurts, but not too much, and also it feels good. The bird's feet are strong. It is holding on to me and I am holding it up.

Come on, says the bird. Let's go.

Dolores cut the woman down. She stunk, like old rotten stew. Her face was blotched and flaccid. She collapsed in an ugly heap on the closet floor.

Dolores thought that was strange. Shouldn't you be stiff if you were dead long enough to smell? But it made the woman a lot easier to handle. All she had to figure out now was what to do with her.

She took her in the bathroom. While hot water ran into the big white tub she removed the woman's clothing. It was basically nondescript: gray sweater, beige and gray and cream plaid skirt. Underwear from Penney's, with comfortable band-sewn legs. Little balls of rolled up lint on the bra. Support pantyhose. Loafers.

Everything from the waist down was soiled. What wasn't smelled like spoiled meat from long, close contact with the corpse. She sat the body on the edge of the tub and guided it gently into the water. It slid so the head was under. She didn't see how that could matter.

While the corpse was soaking she rinsed out the skirt and things in the toilet bowl, thinking how she was going to do this seven more times, if she could find the rest. It was worse than having kids. With them you could use disposables.

She rinsed the dirty clothes out again in the sink, then had to go down to the laundry room to get a basket. She didn't like the basement. It never seemed very clean. Too many things were the same there as outside.

The furnace had long twisting ducts coming out of it, like fat metallic tentacles. Over in the far corner there was a freezer. Nobody used it anymore, not since her mother disappeared. It was chained shut and locked.

When she came back upstairs the body was gone. The water in the tub was clean. She pulled out the stopper by its chain, took the clothes down and loaded them in the machine. Delicate fabrics, short cycle. She left the machine whirring and sloshing away, went to the kitchen and made herself a cup of tea. Then she called up Mrs. Pawkes again, to see if she had any possible clue as to what the hell was going on.

"Well, dear," said Mrs. Pawkes, "I really don't know where I put them all." She raised a be-ringed finger in protest of Dolores' anger. "In my defense—don't frown, you'll make lines, you don't want to end up looking like me, do you?—In my defense I have to say it's mostly because you two *change* the place around so *much*. I mean, I'm sure I could find them, but they're probably not where I put them because where I put them is undoubtedly *gone*, you see . . . " She waited for Dolores to do or say something to show she understood. Dolores nodded tiredly.

"And as far as where they're coming from, Dolores, I really couldn't say."

"You don't have even the slightest idea?"

"Well, it's not the sort of thing . . . " She trailed off again. "It's a delicate subject, I'm afraid. I don't think your father would approve." Dolores thought maybe she should just give up. There were subjects Mrs. Pawkes refused to talk about at all. Sex. Bodily functions. Violence of any sort. That fight two months back, right before her mother had run off—Mrs. Pawkes referred to it as, "That discussion between your parents."

Sometimes Dolores wondered how she ever wound up being their landlady.

"Thanks," she said, hoping she didn't sound too sarcastic. "I'll let you know how it all works out."

His name is Hermie. I know him. I like him, but I don't want to go back. I say no.

He says okay, but it's going to get cold later. Maybe we can find a donut shop. We do. It has a roof like an orange skirt swirling out dancing. The walls are all glass. I wonder if they'll let me in carrying a crow.

Magpie, says Hermie. I am a magpie, not a crow. Anyway, they probably won't even see me.

Why? I ask. I open the door. Hermie is on my shoulder now.

Because I'm a figment of your imagination.

Oh, I say. I thought you were a magpie. It's a joke. I know you can be more than one thing at a time.

Quiet, says Hermie. You don't want them to think you're crazy, do you?

There were dead women all over, once she started looking. Stuffed under the kitchen sink. In the laundry hamper. The pantry. One was wedged in the little space between the fridge and the wall. One was in the spare room, neatly tucked in bed. She had to wash the sheets and mattress pad as well when she did that one's clothes.

They all dissolved in the tub. Their clothes stayed. She had a whole wardrobe of shapeless, baggy, colorless garments on hangers in the laundry room. No two outfits were identical, but they might as well have been. Mix-and-match.

All except the things this one wore. The one she held in her hands. This corpse was only eight or nine inches tall. It still smelled awful. She had found it in the sugar bin.

Washing them got rid of the dead women, but it didn't bring her any closer to the problem's cause. This one was obviously special. Maybe if she did something different this time she could revive it enough to ask it some questions. She thought.

The cookie sheets were in a tall, narrow cupboard made just for them. She rinsed off the heaviest, the best one, while waiting for the oven to pre-heat. Stuck it in for a moment to dry. Took it out and coated it with butter, deciding against a dusting of flour on top of that.

She removed the doll-like clothes and sponged off the small, naked corpse, nervously expecting it to dissolve and disappear. It didn't. She laid the body on the cookie sheet and brushed it with lemon juice. What else? She got some raisins, put two over the dead woman's eyes, one between her slack lips. Was that it? Almost. With a paring knife she cut another raisin in two, then stuck the resulting halves over the nipples. That looked right. The oven was ready. She slid the woman in, set the timer, and put everything away.

I get two fried cakes and a jelly donut. And hot chocolate. It's really good. I hand up crumbs to Hermie where he's still sitting on my shoulder. I giggle and wonder if everybody else just sees pieces of donut disappear into the air. Or maybe they are floating inside Hermie's invisible, imaginary crow-belly.

Magpie, he says, and I laugh out loud.

Am I all right? No.

Nothin' says lovin' like somethin' from the oven. Dolores didn't really need the timer to know when the dead woman was done. The aroma said it all. She smelled kind of good, actually. Kind of—juicy. Delicious, really. Like baked apples. The odor spoke to her invitingly as she pulled out the cookie sheet. She spatulaed up the corpse and transferred it to a cooling rack. Now she'd get some answers.

The dead woman, however, was obstinately silent.

All right, thought Dolores. She reached out and broke off an arm. It tasted sweet and gingery. She closed her eyes to analyze the flavor. Sugar and spice and everything nice. She opened them and saw the pan was empty.

The dead woman must have shinnied down a table leg. She was running across the kitchen floor, headed for the basement steps.

"Oh, no," said Dolores. "Don't go down there." She hurried but she was too late. The little woman fell headlong down the stairs and broke into pieces at the bottom.

Dolores walked down to her carefully, holding on to the rail. Why was she so sad? The other corpses were gone, too, but she'd never cared one way or another about them. She started crying. She picked up the pieces, brushed off some bits of lint.

She took a bite of one big fragment; she thought maybe it was the head. In the far corner the padlocked freezer clicked and hummed to life. Then she remembered.

Two policemen come in. I don't know if I like that. But they just sit down at the other counter, which is this really ugly color like moldy bread. That's why me and Hermie picked the pretty bright orange one on this side.

The man brings them coffee and long, twisty rolls before they even ask for anything. Then he comes back to me again. And I tell him no. No and no and no and no and no. I keep saying no, even after he walks away. Maybe he will get it.

He goes and bothers the police instead. They are talking real quiet and I can't hear the words, but Hermie says uh-oh. I shut up.

One of the police gets off his stool and comes over to me. He calls me ma'am. Do I need help?

I think I better go. It's time to be inside.

Dolores came out. Dolores answered. She said yes. She could use some help. Dolores said there was a problem at her house. She said the policemen should come with her and see. It had to do with the way her mother disappeared a couple of months ago, and how her father had acted ever since. She gave them her name and address, and said she'd be glad to accept their offer of a lift. Yes, it was kind of dangerous being out alone this late.

She wanted to know if they had anything in the squad car that would be good at breaking chains or busting a lock. If not, maybe they ought to stop by the station on the way. She assured them that would be okay. What she wanted to show them was in the freezer. It wasn't going anywhere. It would be all right.

I'm glad Hermie brought me back inside. The policemen were scaring me, and it's good to be home again. He says there won't be any more ghosts to come, either. Dolores made it better.

Dolores is nice. But she always puts away all my toys, and then I have a hard time finding them again. What's left now is my goldfish. I sit down and watch them swimming around and around and around. I wonder if they think they're going anywhere, or if they know what they are in.

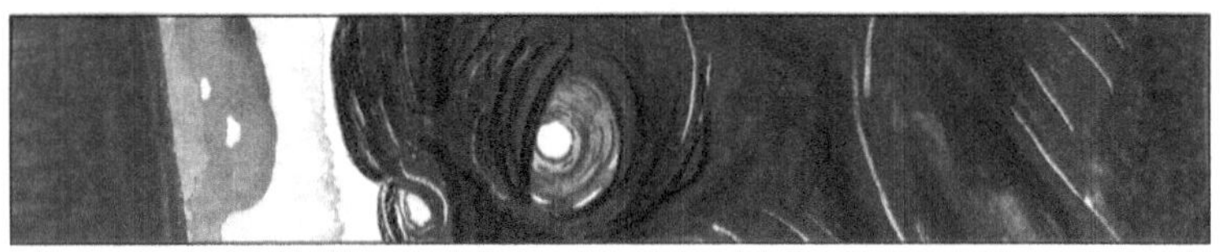

Just Between Us: A Commentary

THIS SHORT AND QUIRKY DARK FANTASY STORY invokes absurd fabulism in its treatment of "dead women" hiding all over the complex where the protagonist lives. Dolores is tasked with cleaning all the mysterious corpses up, when her landlord basically won't do anything about it, and then a bird named Hermie arrives to help find a girl who is missing, and the story gets weirder and weirder from there. I don't want to spoil any of the surprises. Shawl's psychodrama basically splits into the spiritual hunt by the bird for Little Girl and Dolores's attempt to come to terms with what is happening in her complex with all these dead women everywhere… eventually leading to the contents of a mysterious freezer. The final line about the self-awareness of fish in their tank is resonant with potential interpretations for this disturbing tale.

—Michael Arnzen, PhD

At the Huts of Ajala

THEY ALL KEEP CALLING HER A "TWO-HEADED woman." Loanna wants to know why, so after the morning callers leave, she decides on asking her Iya. When she was little, the other kids used to call her "four-eyes." But this is different, said with respect by grown adults.

She finds the comb and hair-grease on the bureau in the room where she's been sleeping. When she left Cleveland three days ago, it was winter. Now she steps out onto the wrought-iron balcony, and it's spring. Her first visit, on her own, to the Crescent City, New Orleans, drowning home of her mother's kin.

Iya sits in her wicker chair, waiting. She is a tall woman, even seated, and she's dressed all in white: white headscarf, white blouse, white skirt with matching belt, white stockings and tennis shoes, and a white cardigan, too, which she removes now that the day has warmed. She shifts her feet apart, and Loanna drops to sit between them.

Certainly Loanna is old enough to do her own hair, but Iya knows different ways of braiding, French rolls and corn rows, special styles suitable for the special occasion of a visit to Mam'zelle La Veau's grave. Besides, it's nice to feel Iya's hands, her long brown fingers gently nimble, swiftly touching, rising along the length of Loanna's wiry tresses and transforming them into neat, uniformly bumpy braids. Relaxed by the rhythm and intimacy, she asks, "Why all your friends call me that?"

"Call you what, baby?" Iya's voice is rough but soft, like a terrycloth towel. "Hand me up a bobby-pin."

"Two-headed," says Loanna. She lifts the whole card full of pins and feels the pressure as her Iya chooses one and pulls it free.

"Two-headed? It means like you got the second sight, sorta. Like Indian mystics be talkin' about openin' they third eye. Only more so."

"But why say it like that?" Loanna asks, persisting. Some odd things have gone on since she got here: folks dropping on one knee, saying prayers in African to the dry, exacting sound of rattling gourds. Tearful entrances and laughing retreats, gifts of honey, candles, and coconuts. Not every question gets her an answer, but she's here to learn, so she always tries again. "Why call it two-headed, and why say that about me?"

"Oooh, now that's a story." Iya pauses for a moment, finishing off a row, and the murmur of a neighbor's voice rises through slow rustling trees and over the courtyard wall, light and indistinct. Iya sections off another braid, and repeats herself. "That is *truly* a *story*, baby. You wanna hear it now?"

Loanna nods, then winces from the pain of pulling her own hair. "*Ow*! I mean, yeah," she says.

"*Try* to sit still, then, so I can concentrate. Lessee. This story started before you were born, Loanna, 'bout fifteen years ago. The night before you were born, actually, to be exact. You remember that night?"

"Naww," says Loanna, giggling.

"Your mama sure do. But she ain't the only one. I was *there*, and what I can't tell you ain't nobody can. Here, shift yourself this way so I can reach the back. You comfortable?"

Loanna scoots the pillow forward. "Mmm-hmm." She faces a peach stucco wall now, not so interesting as the view she had had of the garden. So Loanna closes her eyes, lets her Iya's words form pictures in her mind.

This is what she sees—

She sees herself. She sees Loanna-that-was, Loanna-to-come, Loanna-she-who-will-always-be. She can tell by her feet, large like her mama's, by her strong, long, legs. She can tell by her milk-and-honey skin. (How'd she get to be so fair? No white folks, counting back for five generations... but that's another story.) She recognizes her flat butt that reminds her daddy of Aunt Fiona, and there's the mark like two lips above it; Aunt Nono calls that an Angel's Kiss. Her back looks funny; maybe that's because she never really gets to see it. Her breasts look bigger. She can see them swaying in and out of sight as she walks away from her own disembodied point of view, down some sort of path.

But her breasts aren't the *main* difference. The *main* difference is her head. Or the lack of it; her head is not there. In its place are rays of shimmering light that stream down from a luminous ball floating nearly a foot above the stem of her graceful neck. The ball of light itself is colorless, but as Loanna's viewpoint follows it she sees it sending flares of color in all directions. She understands from her Iya that this is her *ori,* which contains instructions and wisdom from the ancestors. With the guidance of her ori she has left the heavenly city, on her way to choose a head. It is a very important decision.

Coming too quickly around a turn in the path, she catches up with herself, suddenly merging with the ball of light. All at once, it is as if she has a thousand eyes. Each beam of light absorbs the significance of what it touches, in a depth and detail Loanna has difficulty handling. Images spin into her out of the formerly indistinguishable darkness: the stern trunks of trees stand in meaningful positions; their beckoning branches droop with leaves, each leaf a poem, waiting to fall with a sigh, reciting itself as it drifts free. But the piercing rays need not wait as they caress each layer of cellular structure, reading the secrets of greenness and sugar, tasting chlorophyll and acknowledging Loanna's part in its manufacture, her gaseous contribution to its growth. Then there is the throb and rustle of waves of wind, then the shift to shooting through the soil beneath her feet, which is alive: warm and changing with worms, and damp and seething with nameless hungers that are hers, it's all hers, all herself.

Somehow, she adjusts. She swims in the sea of the knowledge of everything around her. She wears an apron of fine cowrie shells (*caressing tides of food; soft, sucking feet*), a skirt of grass (*dry whispers of a burning sun*), a leather pouch—she tries to absorb it all. Directed by her *ori*, she even manages to move forward, toward her destiny. Wonders around her part and let her pass.

There is sand beneath her feet (*silica, each grain a window in a castle on another world*) and a curtain of vines before her (*twisting, the eternal spiral up, and drinking from a hidden well*) when she reaches the place to which she has been led. She peers through the leaves and *sees* a fire-lit clearing (*the shape of a spicy scent in the wood burning, a curl of smoke—the eternal spiral up*). Over the fire hangs a kettle (*the song of its making rings like a silent gong in the play of her vision*) filled with bubbling stew (*reluctant roots dug and diced apart, farewells from the nervous forager which gave its body, its blood*).

Ajala, the maker of heads, enters the clearing. He is like a man. A drunk man, Loanna perceives. A mean drunk. He has lost, gambling. Lost to the King, a spirit of swords and justice. The cowries clicked and fell, clicked and fell, all day, till he was without a shell to pay. This is all Loanna can tell from a single "glance." Another ray streams out in his direction—and Ajala seizes it as it lands! He is no man, but a god! He pulls her forward by the ray of her perception.

She stands in front of Ajala. He is dark and crooked (*the better to become lost in*) and not at *all* in a happy mood (*a woman wrapped her goods in white cloth and walked away*). He *speaks* to her, laying heavy slabs of speech upon her mind. He gives her anger, wet and cynically cold, which would mean this in words: "Ha, you come too late! You seek a head? I have ceased to make heads. What is the use, when they will all eventually belong to the King? Not even those already made will I sell to you, for with the rise of the sun all will belong to him, to Kabio Sile. And I am too drunk to bring you to them now. Besides, I want my stew. You are welcome to join me—except, of course, you have no mouth!"

Unkind laughter fills the clearing. Loanna turns to go, switching her hips angrily, which causes her cowrie shell apron to clatter. Ajala stops her with one hand on her shoulder and swings her back around.

"But what is this?" says Ajala. "You are *very rich*! With these beautiful shells I could cancel my debt! Very well, I will take you. But just to the F hut, no farther."

The F hut . . . this is where he stores those heads barely worthy of the name. Loanna is sure the ancestors have provided her with enough goods for a C, the next grade up. But even an F is better than nothing, she figures. So she removes the apron, and he receives it, and they are off.

Stars have appeared above them. The *ori* touches their colors with its own and brings to Loanna their distance, their magnificently pure combustion and their blazing bravery of the void. Then she is at the F hut, and it is time to choose.

These heads are made of mud, and they are really pretty bad. Some of them aren't even dry yet. The features are all rough and mostly irregular in size and shape. As she squats to turn the mud heads over and pick the best, the leather pouch swings out on its cord, then bangs against her belly. It sobs of lost herdmates, of running open-nosed, into the wind—but what's within?

Curious, she pulls it open, puts in her fingers and draws out a pinch of salt (*longing for the cresting waves, shh, the hissing of the sea, exposed before the sun now, but once, what is it that lies at the bottom of the ocean?*). Ah, here is the rest of her fortune! Perhaps she can obtain a C head after all.

Ajala waits impatiently for her decision—too impatiently, it seems to Loanna. She picks an F at random, lifts it, makes as though to put it on. There is an angle, a hidden aspect to Ajala's waiting that is somehow wrong. His eyes are growing strangely larger as he watches her lower the head. They are almost all he has now for a face: huge eyes watching as she lowers the head over her ori. But what is this terrible blankness descending upon her mind? The telling colors cannot penetrate the thick mud of her head—it is a trap! Quickly she raises the F back up and sets it to the side. Ajala leans over her, silent yet threatening. She throws her hands up in defense, and two grains of salt fly from her fingers to his face. Of course they land in his enormous eyes. Tears spill from them and fall upon the ground. Ajala cries (*no love, alone, alone, no one, no love*). When he is finished he sighs wistfully. His sigh says, "It is too long since I've had the salt to spare for tears. Is there more?"

Loanna shows him the pouchful. Good. In exchange for the salt, he will take her to choose a C head. Through the songs of insects (*brief, brief, but sharp and fleet is our short leap, bright, sweet, the glittering of our span*) and the heavy dew they go, to come at last to the C hut.

These heads are made of woven wood. There is a certain uniformity of feature. They're better than the F heads, but there's nothing spectacularly exciting about any of them. Because she sees no real differences, Loanna chooses quickly. Before putting on her C head she checks out Ajala. He is withdrawn, brooding over his many ancient wrongs and sorrows. No trick this time, it seems. The head fits smoothly into place.

She can't see. It is dark. She can smell the soil, hear the crickets, but it is all filtered, lessened to the trickle of experience that she used to be used to. The rays of her ori tease her with flickering glimpses of the essence. She turns, blinks her eyelids, parts her lips experimentally. "I—" she says, a creaking in the night. The crickets silence themselves. "I want—" She wants an A head. An *A*. But she doubts this bitter god will grant her wish for the asking. And she has used up all the trade goods the ancestors gave her, just to reach the point where she realizes that what she wants is *more*.

She'll have to use what she's been given to get what must be gotten, then.

There. That darker darkness must be he. She addresses it. "I want—to thank you from the bottom of my heart. I mean like, this is so completely swollen! I thought you said you were only gonna give me a C head. But this A is—is—it's—"

The god appears clearly before her, shining with anger. It lights him as though it were a fire, and he glows like a maddened furnace. "It is a C! A C head is what you have and nothing but a C!"

Loanna fears the heat of Ajala's anger will ignite her poor wooden head. Also she feels something she's never felt before, a sort of... tugging... at the top. But she persists. "Oh, chill, it's all right," she says. "I'll let everybody know what a deal I got. Unless—" holding up a hand to forestall further wrath, "unless you don't want me to. No, okay, I won't tell. You made some kinda mistake, *dincha*?"

Ajala strives to control his anger. He succeeds in subduing himself to a dull red glow. "This is the C hut. It contains nothing but C heads!"

"Uhh, yeah. Sure. I understand. I won't tell anybody. Except if they notice and ask me how I got it, okay?"

"*Aarrgh!*" bellows Ajala. "Come!" He grabs her with one hot hand and drags her into the forest.

There is no path; at least none that Loanna can detect. The way is a lot more difficult and a lot less interesting than the last two trips. Just stumbling through the dark, her hand sweating in the hot grip of the god's. She'd probably be a little steadier on her feet if it wasn't for the insistent tugging at her scalp, pulling her constantly off course.

After a while, the darkness lessens. This seems to increase Ajala's fury. Without warning he stops, picks Loanna up by the waist, and flings her over his shoulder. Then he's off again, at an uncomfortable trot.

"What's… the big… hurry?" she manages to whuff out between the god's jolting strides.

"Dawn," he explains. Between panting breaths he adds "I must… return soon… to pay my debt… to the King… or lose my heads. But first… you will see… you are wrong. Not far now," he ends.

By the time they reach the A hut, Loanna's neck is sore from the odd tugging, which has for the most part been perpendicular to their path. The rest of her feels a little rough as well. And she feels even worse when she sees the A heads.

These heads are made of jewels.

Amethyst, rose quartz, aventurine, and other stones she cannot name, they glow with living light. Each is perfect, each unique. There is no way to pretend that what she wears is one of these. So much for deceit.

What else does she have? She has spent her inheritance. She has used her head, such as it is. She kneels before the luminous beauty of the As, but she's being pulled away by this unaccountable vacuum. What *is* it?

"Mama!" she screams in fear and frustration. "*Maa-maa!*"

And that's when she gets it: the answer to her question and the solution to her problem, too, all at once, all in one. Where she's going, where she'll soon be coming from. The door, the gate, the entranceway for everything that ever was in the world.

"Wait," she pleads to the unseen force. "Mama, wait just a minute. I got a idea." Her mother must hear her, or *some*body must, for the compelling pressure to be born lessens just a little.

"Ajala," she says. "You got the cowries. You got the salt. But you'd like more, right? Course you would. For an A head I—"

"You admit you have only a C head?"

"Yeah, well, I guess I did try to jack you around a little. Sorry. But now, if you let me choose an A head I can lead you to the source. Where I got the shells and cowries *from*. Take away as much as you can carry!"

"Is it far? I don't have much time . . . "

"No, no, it's really close. It'll only take a few minutes, okay? Can I pick one?"

Ajala nods. Breathlessly, she selects a large, round head of pale blue celestite. There is a moment of disorientation as she removes her C and is flooded by the universe (*the turning, rising rightly, the eternal helix up*). But then the celestite is over her ori, focusing and altering her perceptions, directing and filtering the rays of light that connect her to the world: her awareness of that connection. Plus she has her other senses: eyes, ears, nose; all working very well. Is that faint odor fish?

Ajala looks different through these eyes. Loanna decides that she now finds him cooler. She stands and beckons him to come and kneel before her. Parting her skirt, she brings him gently to the source.

The god is reverent. He prays to the source, mouthing soundless words. He speaks skillfully, with a silver tongue.

Loanna sags against him, pliable with pleasure. She is pulled taut again, stretched between these two irresistible forces: one between her legs, the other somewhere over her shoulders.

At last she can stand no more. "I like your approach," she says softly. "Now let's see your retreat." To her surprise he backs away without protest. He looks up at her, smiling happily. A huge pearl falls from his lips; his reward.

She has to go. She really must. But as she is drawn away from the A hut, out into her life, Ajala places the C head into her hands (long fingers like her grandfather's, but they don't look a bit artistic on top of Uncle Donald's square palms).

She is confused by the god's offering. "Put it on," he says in a receding shout. "Put it on, wear it over your A. You can always take it off again. And you may find it necessary, sometimes, to be less than you are capable of being. I know—"

His last words are lost as she is born.

Loanna opens her eyes. Shadows sway on the stucco wall, struck by the lowering sun. The lingering sweetness of the god's homage spreads like syrup through the afternoon air, mingling with the golden light. Her dream of the story is over, though Iya's voice continues, twisting its ends together, pulling them up and into the eternal spiral.

"Yeah, we finally got you to make up your mind to honor us with your presence, and you came all in a rush into this world," Iya finishes. "I was hot and dizzy from all that bendin' up and down, all that runnin' back and forth. Didn't nobody offer *me* no ice chips. But I got to see you first, and right away, and I knew you were special. A caul, yeah, but that don't automatically mean that much." Iya pauses. Her swift fingers lie still in her lap, their task long done. "It was your eyes told me. Told me everything I just told you—and then some. I can't remember everything your eyes told me on the day that you was born."

"So then was when you decided you were gonna teach me?"

"When you was old enough, right," Iya says. "So let's get on off this balcony and go visit Mam'zelle La Veau. You got the coins? Your *gele's* on the bed, with the rest of your outfit. We'll pick us up some flowers for the gravesite on the way. Anything else your ori's tellin you to bring, baby?"

Loanna's eyes close again, enabling her to focus on the resonance within, the quiet bell of her consciousness. "A—a egg? A *blue* egg?! Iya, how we supposed to get that?"

Iya rolls her eyes. "Honey, I don' know. But if the ancestors tellin' you Mam'zelle need a blue egg, we gone get her a blue egg."

"But, Iya, don't you think it might—"

"Loanna!" Iya's voice is sharp and stern. "Here's the first thing you gotta learn: when your head tells you somethin', *listen.* 'Specially if you askin' a question. You get an answer, accept that answer." She rises and holds out her hands to help her student stand.

"Today you prayin' for the help and guidance of a woman who was famous for not takin' nothin' off nobody, the original Voodoo Queen. So you gotta be sincere, and you gotta stand firm for yourself. Like when we buy our flowers and you give the man a twenty dollar bill, and if he only give you change back for a ten, what you gonna do?"

Loanna's fingers trace the braids curving above her ears. "Ask him where's the rest. 'Cause I know I'm not stupid. I can count."

"That's right. Same way with this. You know. You not stupid. That's what you gotta learn to believe, honey, you wanna live up to your potential. After all," Iya concludes as Loanna follows her inside, "what's the good of havin' two heads unless you use 'em?"

At the Huts of Ajala: A Commentary

"AT THE HUTS OF AJALA" IS A SURREAL TALE OF female empowerment. It takes the reader on an amazing journey into a spiritual realm as only Nisi Shawl can describe it, drawing from the wells of African folklore and vodun to generate unique imagery, all of it summoned to tell a strong feminist tale.

Generally, it's the story of a young girl coming of age spiritually by showing how she navigates and outwits a trickster god. The tale is framed as an origin story told by a godmother, Iya, to Loanna about the spiritual events leading up to her birth; but the story succeeds in representing the spiritual side of vodun through the direct subjective experience of Loanna as she envisions the story she is told... which ends up being a kind of *narrative birthing* represented as a crossing over from the mythic realm to the physical. It is easy to neglect the frame narrative of Iya's storytelling, but it's important because it establishes this narrative as not only a woman's story, but also an African *Woman's* story, cutting across generational lines.

Loanna's initial question about why she's two-headed drives the theme of the story. The answer is not simply that there are several heads one can receive from the gods, but that Lo won't settle for the subordinate "C" head they want to give her. Through sassiness and seduction, she gathers two heads from Ajala—both a bejeweled and beautiful "A" head and the common "C"—and wears one over the other... suggesting perhaps that she can play against the binaries of the world by switching them as needed. As Loanna herself mentions within the story, "She'll have to use what she's been given to get what must be gotten." The story is essentially about choice and encourages autonomy.

—Michael Arnzen, PhD

Street Worm

DOWN, DOWN, DOWN: DUST AND MUD AND mortar and steel plunged story upon story into the earth. Brit Williams clung to the chain link fence surrounding the construction site as if only the desperate strength of her thin brown fingers kept her from falling in.

She could see the pit's bottom—barely. Late afternoon in Seattle during the first week of February meant darkness owned the corners, shadows filled in all the low places and rose like dirty water to hide everything, eventually, even . . .

Dragging her eyes up along the building's still-exposed girders and beams, Brit spotted the giant nest, shining gray and silver in the last of the twilight. She hunched smaller in her good leather coat. But as far as she knew, the worm-like things that lived between those web walls couldn't see her.

"You all right, kid?"

The cops sure could, though. "Yeah," she lied, meeting the policewoman's eyes. White people liked that. "Just wanted a look before I got on the bus home." Did that sound suspicious? Had she said too much?

No. The cop let her walk downhill and cross the intersection without interference. She strode briskly into the cold drizzle as if she really did have somewhere to go.

Well, she did. If she'd only admit to her parents she was crazy, she could go home. She could fit herself right back into their careful, bougie lives.

Except she was sane. Brit was pretty sure of that.

No one else seemed to see the nests, though. Whereas for her they were everywhere. Heading north on First Ave she walked by three, all stuck to the sides of skyscrapers in the throes of renovation. People going the other way faced her and passed on, oblivious office workers and ignorant drunks. The traffic light ahead changed and Brit hurried out into the street to get away from a close one hanging only a few floors above the sidewalk. Behind the nest's pale sides, paler shapes writhed disgustingly, knotting together and sliding apart—she stopped to watch in fascination till a rough jolt to her shoulder and a muttered curse got her moving again. On the street's other side she checked her pants' front pocket. Her cash was still there.

But the clerk at the Green Tortoise Hostel wouldn't take it.

Brit tried. She showed him she really had enough money, laying a wrinkled twenty on the greasy counter and smoothing it out flat. The man shook his shaggy head like a refugee from a Scooby-Doo cartoon.

"Nope. Not without proper ID."

Brit glared at him. She'd shown him that, too. "What ain't proper about—" She slapped her hand down on her fake driver's license fast, grabbing it back before he could confiscate it. His large hand rested awkwardly between them.

"Look, do you need help? Somewhere to stay the night?"

Wasn't that what she'd wanted to pay him for? If she hadn't been so damn short, he might not have asked how old she was. Lots of people told Brit she acted four, even five years older than her age. She could have passed for eighteen, easily—if she stood a little taller. But no.

"Problems at home? Let me call somebody—" He turned for the phone behind him and Brit bolted back outside.

Getting dark. The rain had slacked off, but the cold felt worse. At least she couldn't smell Shaggy's stale cigarette butts anymore.

She took in a deep breath, convincing herself she was better off. So much for Plan A. Plan B was more flexible. Okay, less well-formed. The basics were the same: Stay away from her parents till they gave up labeling her "disturbed." Skip the appointment they'd made for her tomorrow afternoon with a psychiatrist.

She plodded stoically uphill. East. And south, away from the Green Tortoise. The library would probably still be open, but Brit wasn't in the mood to read. Too hungry. She pushed open the door of the Hotel Monaco's restaurant and went in.

Warm air caressed her, carrying in its soft swirls the aromas of fresh bread, baked herbs and onions, roasting meat—

"May I help you?" The way the woman walking toward her spoke made it clear she didn't think helping Brit was in her power or anyone else's. Brit had eaten here before. Only lunch, though. Everybody on that shift was used to her, but obviously she was just another black kid to this high-heeled blonde. And obviously she was too young to be eating dinner alone. "Meeting another party?"

Brit's gaze swept around the room. The only other customers were a couple of old ladies in red and purple suits and bizarrely flowered hats. "Yeah. S'pozed to be. Look like I'm early."

Mostly Brit talked the way she did to make Mom and Dad angry. Ebonics didn't fit in with their image as "professionals." Of course it pissed off her friend Iyata's mother Sylvie, too, but that only meant they had to meet at school half the time. Not such a hardship. And maybe the use of Ebonics reminded the blonde it was National Brotherhood Week or something: she showed Brit to a nice table and gave her a menu without any more questions.

She ordered a cup of tea to drink while she was "waiting." She sipped it slowly, trying to figure out what story she'd tell to explain why the imaginary adults didn't show up for their ostensible rendezvous with her. She'd need to fake a phone call . . .

The outside door opened again and she glanced up exactly as if she really was expecting to meet someone here. In came a round-bellied white man in a navy blue coat, his long gray hair in a ponytail. Probably friends with the two old ladies. "There she is!" he said, brushing past the hostess and heading straight for Brit. Not the old ladies. Brit.

"How's my little half-pint of cider half drunk up?" The strange man smiled and plopped down in her table's other chair. "Play along!" he whispered. "Pretend you know me till I get a chance to—"

"Ready to order?" The waiter had appeared from nowhere to stand by the table at attention. He had a green notepad in his hands and a mildly worried expression on his face.

Brit could get up and scream for him to call the cops. That'd be great—they'd take her right back home. Besides, this table-crasher guy suddenly looked familiar. She narrowed her eyes. An actor? It was coming back to her: the race-flipped production that The Conciliation Project had brought to her school—"Uncle Tom?"

One of the man's bushy eyebrows lifted. "Don't look so surprised! Didn't you get our message? Aunt Eliza came down with the flu and sent me by myself." He turned to the waiter as if just noticing him. "I'd like a Jungle Bird, if the bar's open."

"Yes, sir!" The waiter left, looking reassured.

When they were alone again "Uncle Tom" hunched forward and laid his arms on the table. "Thanks," he said. "That was pretty brave of you."

"Yeah, well, get any nearer and I'm leavin'."

"Fair enough." He leaned back. "I guess I ought to be grateful you recognized me—from that play version of *Uncle Tom's Cabin*, I take it?"

Brit nodded. "But that don't mean I trust you no further than I can throw the chair you sittin' in."

"Fair enough," he said again. The waiter returned carrying a glass round as the man's belly, full of ice and an orangey liquid. A section of a pineapple ring gripped its rim. He left again after taking their orders: lasagna for Brit, which was what she usually had at lunch, and quail for her supposed uncle.

"All right, before we're interrupted anymore, let me try to tell you what I'm doing talking to you. Did you ever read—or see—*The Shining*?"

Brit was tired of white people assuming she was stupid simply because she was dark-skinned. Another reason she'd started talking hood; before, they always said how she was so *articulate*. "I can read!"

"Never said you couldn't. Lots of kids don't bother with books, though; young people nowadays seem to prefer movies. Anyway, the book and the movie *are* different: the Scatman Crothers character doesn't die at the end of the novel. But what both versions of the story got right was how some of us, some of us who can do special things, have this glow to us, this 'shining' if you will . . . like you."

Like her. "You sayin' I'm magic?"

"For lack of a better word, yes. Yes I am."

"How 'bout 'insane'? How 'bout 'hallucinatin''?" She was standing—her legs shook. She hoped it didn't show. She kept her voice low. "How 'bout 'depressed an delusional'? All kinda things people be sayin' I am, an ain't none of 'em good—" On the edge of her field of vision she saw the waiter approaching with a basket of bread.

"Ima' go the bathroom. When I come out you be gone." She picked up her backpack from where she'd dropped it and fled.

"Wait, let me finish—"

She slammed the restroom door behind her and turned on the water so she wouldn't have to hear what he was saying. Peed, wiped, flushed, washed her hands. Eyes on the mirror, she pulled out her pick and went to work on her short little fro. Then a touch-up to her liner and mascara—Mom and Dad didn't allow her to wear make-up, but Brit kept a supply for use away from home.

She took a long time, but when she emerged the man—she didn't even know his real name!—was sitting where she'd left him. Between her and the exit. He stood up as she walked by—he didn't attempt to stop her, though. All he did was say, "Sorry. I don't blame you for being scared."

That made her turn around. "I ain't scared!"

"No? Then maybe you'll sit down and eat quietly with me?"

Brit suddenly noticed that the hostess, the waiter, the old ladies—everyone in the whole restaurant was staring at her. She didn't need that kind of attention. With an angry look at "Uncle Tom" she sat back in her abandoned chair.

"Maybe put on a slightly less murderous expression?"

Brit closed her eyes and took three deep breaths like her dad was always counseling his clients to do. When she opened them there was a white card on the table in front of her. "Elias Crofutt" read the first line, in a flowing, cursive-like script. Below it, in much plainer letters: "Theater, Language, Hierophance"—whatever *that* was. Below those words was a phone number. All printed in dark purple ink.

"Ken Rodriguez—at the hostel—called my pager after you left so—precipitously."

Shaggy. "He had one a these?" she asked. "Why come?"

"Often there's trouble at home when a talent such as yours emerges. I keep an eye out for kids at risk, and I have my contacts in likely spots watching for—"

"You got spies? You a nasty fuckin' creeper!" Brit scraped her seat away from the table.

"Wait! Don't you want to know how I found you?"

Yes she did. The Green Tortoise was eight blocks away, too far for mere coincidence. And she'd never heard of this sort of operation in Seattle. Both her parents worked with teens—Dad as a psychiatrist, Mom as a social worker. It was why they were so sure they knew what was wrong with her. They were always warning her about things she'd never be enough of an idiot to get mixed up in; surely they would have mentioned running across a scheme like this? What if she could tell them about something they'd missed? That would make her look on top of everything—completely sane. She nodded cautiously.

"I was trying to tell you: you *shine*. I followed your light—" He stopped midsentence. The waiter brought salads and set them on the table in the abrupt, awkward silence.

Brit smothered her lettuce and carrot chips in ranch and picked up her fork, determined to get some food in her stomach. She'd been too busy arguing with her mom to eat this afternoon at home. "You was sayin'." She crammed a loaded fork in her mouth.

"I keep an office at the Y."

So cross off staying there. That put a big dent in Plan B.

"When I called Kenny back he described you—not only what you were wearing but—well, it's like invisible fireworks coming out of the top of your head—"

"*Riiight.*" Let the man spew out his new age sewage. She would concentrate on getting some nourishment under her belt. One forkful at a time.

"I know how this sounds. Believe me. Or maybe it's more like sparklers than fireworks, because you leave a trail in the air for a minute or two . . . Well. Anyway. *I* can see it, though most can't."

Grimly, Brit swallowed and began chewing a third mouthful of crunchy, oil-coated salad. Plan C was even hazier in her mind than B. And this dude was seriously woo-woo.

Or maybe not. If she was sane, he could be, too. Maybe? Would he back her up? Would her parents believe him? Or would they call him nuts—politely—to his face?

The waiter came back with their entrees before she could decide. Steam wafted off her lasagna when she cut apart the crusty cheesy top layer. Too hot to eat yet. "What my fireworks look like?" she asked.

"White and gold with flecks of ruby-red," Crofutt replied promptly. Not hesitating as if he was making stuff up. "I've never seen anything quite like it."

"That mean you don't know what kinda magic I do?"

"Correct. But I can help you figure it out. If you need me to." He sliced meat off the quail's breast and ate a couple of bites before he spoke again. "Anything else you need, just ask. Money, weapons, somewhere to stay the night . . . "

There was being scared and then there was being smart. She flagged the waiter down. "Put this in a go box," she said, gesturing at her food. She dug out the same bill she'd offered Shaggy. Kenny. It ought to cover her share. Plus tip.

"Through already?"

Brit stood up and the man didn't try to stop her. "So through." She kept her voice low so no one else would notice her anger. "Here some cash to pay for my food. You can see I don't need your stinkin' money. Don't need you runnin' crystals up an' down my body, neither, or whatever freaky thing get you off before you stranglin' me—"

"No! You're wrong!" Crofutt protested. "Sit down—*please*!"

"I ain't!" She tilted her head to one side and grinned ferociously for the benefit of the waiter coming back with her boxed up lasagna. "Tell Aunt Eliza I hope she be better for church Sunday," she said, too sweetly. "Thanks for the offer, but I gotta go." She swung her pack onto her left shoulder, took the box from the waiter, and headed for the door.

Behind her Brit heard the white man getting up and following her. She made it almost to the door before she felt his touch on her coat sleeve. She whirled fast and he dropped the offending hand.

But he held the other out to give her the card from the table. "You almost forgot this."

Rather than attract more attention she took it and shoved it in her coat pocket. "Good *night.*"

"Be careful!" he shouted as she stepped outside. "It's—"

The door banged shut and cut the last words off. Full night had fallen and a freezing wind blew off the bay.

There was one spot Brit knew would be probably a little warmer. And empty. Not somewhere safe, exactly, but she was out of other options. She walked downhill again and turned north on Third to avoid the Green Tortoise. She wasn't paranoid; she didn't really think Shaggy would even know she was going by the building. It was just better not to take any chances.

She wasn't paranoid. Something told her to look back up the street at Third, though, and here came Crofutt, striding after her as fast as his fat self could go. Which was surprisingly fast.

The second door past the corner had an "Open" sign hanging behind its glass. Brit yanked it out of the way and hurried inside. She put a couple of rows of shelves between her and the window before she came to a halt.

This was a cigar store. A pretty swanky one, too. Shelves and shelves of boxes full of brown cylinders: fat, thin, dark, light, short, long, banded in gold, wrapped in cellophane, as various as people.

"May I help you?" The man asking that question this time sounded as if he might really want to. He looked nice, too. He had curly, medium long hair, black mixed with silver; smooth skin the color of one of his cigars; a nose curved like a bird's beak; a mustache lifted up at its ends by his smile.

"My dad birthday comin' up," she improvised. Actually, that wouldn't be till June. "I wanna get him somethin' extra cool."

"Of course. He is already a smoker? A connoisseur? I may know him. What's his name?"

"He only started 'round Christmas." What a tangled web. Would she have to make up a reason why he'd started then?

With a few more lies Brit stretched the visit out to half an hour. She bought a gold-plated cigar trimmer, a bead-covered lighter shaped like a butterfly, and six of the hugest cigars she could find. That took two of her hundreds.

It was worth it, though. When she left the shop there was no sign of Crofutt the Creeper. She continued north toward the Denny Triangle neighborhood, then walked east again on Stewart to Westlake, keeping out of the Belltown bar scene.

The crowds dwindled and disappeared. Someday, Mom said, this part of town was going to get bought up and gentrified. Meanwhile it was home mostly to what the planning commissions her parents monitored called "light industry": newspaper offices, award plaque engravers, embroidery factories, etc. Low brick buildings, their walls dull with old paint, all dark and empty now. Including the one where Brit was going to have to spend the night.

Kind of ironic, she thought, keeping her eyes on the ground as she walked the final yards to the building's back entrance. Her fight with Mom and Dad had been all about not coming anywhere near this place they bought for a teen center. No way. But here she was.

She would probably be okay. As long as she didn't look up.

The realtor's lockbox still dangled from the dead fluorescent lamp beside the door. Her parents didn't know she knew the combination. The key was still inside it.

The key undid the lock easily. The door creaked. Only a little, though. Could the giant wriggly things on the rooftop even hear anything?

Brit peered inside. Gray-blue squares glowed dimly on the floor where the city's faint light had funneled in via the high, dirty windows. The pale patches wavered like reflections. A real hallucination? No.

The floor was underwater.

Brit stepped cautiously in. The linoleum beneath the rubber soles of her Converse shoes squelched as if it was wet, but at least she didn't hear her feet full-on splashing. Not deep enough, maybe? She shut the door and felt in her pack for her flashlight.

Crouching, she aimed the light low, hoping no one would see it. Nearby, the beige tiles she remembered from her first reluctant visit glittered only faintly, as if covered in sweat. But in the wide room's middle, the row of poles supporting its ceiling rose from a shallow pool.

As she walked around the room's edge, Brit's mood sank lower and lower. Tops, there was maybe half an inch of water anywhere, but it went almost from wall to wall. Not real comfortable to sleep in. Her bag would be soaked in no time, wherever she put it down.

Four doors led off the main room on its far side. The first opened on a closet. She felt its floor to be sure. Dripping wet. The second and third doors were locked. The outside key didn't work on them.

The fourth door was locked, too—but with the deadbolt's knob on *this* side. Behind it a stair climbed up to a dark landing.

Brit frowned. From what she remembered, this place had just one story. Arriving on the landing she looked up from there and saw that the stairs stopped at a metal fire door with a push bar for its handle.

A door onto the roof. Where an enormous tent full of worms waited.

She couldn't go there. Anyway, outside she'd be cold and, if the rain came back, just as wet as lying on the flooded floor below. With a sigh she scuffed back down to the landing. Tiny, but so was she. She unrolled her bag and fluffed it out, slipped inside. Her coat folded up into a big pillow. She tucked it under her head and waited.

The landing was concrete. Dry. Hard. Dad said it took the

average person fourteen minutes to fall asleep. She waited some more. And some more. And some more.

She checked her watch and sure enough she'd stayed awake a lot longer than fourteen minutes. Maybe she needed more padding. She opened her coat up and put it under the bag. Now she didn't have a pillow—her pack was too lumpy, filled with pretend birthday presents. She shouldn't crush the cigars. That left—her lasagna! She must have dropped it somewhere—no use trying to figure out the exact spot now. But with nothing else to do she backtracked mentally anyway and decided she'd left the box balanced on the rim of a trashcan when she re-tied her shoelaces. Maybe she was too hungry to sleep.

Maybe it was too early: only 8, and she usually went to bed around 9 on a school night.

She switched from cradling her head on her left arm to her right.

No use going back over the fight with Mom, either, thinking of what she should have said. Like, "Why don't you trust me? Why don't you believe me?" Like, "Just because all the other teenagers you deal with are on drugs doesn't mean I have the same problem." Like, "I am *not* insane!"

Instead, after a while, she'd given up saying anything. Talking wasn't going to do any good. Brit decided she was simply going to have to disappear. Actions spoke louder than words. She would take off; that way she'd miss school, miss the "counseling" appointment scheduled right afterward, miss her parents picking her up from there to drag her along to the infested building they'd bought.

So how ridiculous was it that she'd wound up spending the night in the same building, practically right next to a worm nest after all, on her own? Alone? In the dark?

Well, coming here hadn't been her first idea. Or even her second.

The problem was, everyone in Seattle who was supposed to help kids knew her mom and dad. Now she had a chance to think, a bus or a train ride seemed like her best option. To Yakima or Spokane, or somewhere no one would look. Soon as it got light she'd walk to the station. Before school started, so she'd be less suspicious.

But if she was going to leave town early tomorrow morning she'd better get to sleep soon. She checked her watch again. 10:00. Past time. Her alarm would start beeping at 6. She put the watch back away in her pencil bag and zipped that in a pocket she never used so it would be harder to find and hit snooze. Shoved her pack a couple of stairs up so she'd have further to reach for it. But she could still hear it ticking.

Except her watch was digital.

It didn't tick.

Had someone followed her in? How? She *knew* she'd locked the door. And there hadn't been any other way—she'd gone all around everywhere. Except for those two locked doors.

She pulled the pack back down to the landing and held it to her ear to be sure. Nothing. Let go of it and listened again. Louder, now, and faster. And coming from above—the opposite direction of whatever was behind the doors. And faster. And louder. Like a shower of rocks. Like a storm of hail—was that it? A storm? Maybe she should retreat to the ground floor for safety. A hurricane could rip an old building like this apart—there hadn't been any predictions of a storm that bad, though. Had there?

She needed to see. But the worms were up there. Did the noise come from them? What were they doing?

She could find out looking from the street. She put her shoes on and grabbed the key and her flashlight. She turned that off at the bottom of the stairs for a moment and immediately stepped in a stray puddle. Great.

Sticking near the wall she reached the front door without further mishap. And of course it was locked like she'd left it.

But the ticking noise was loud, even down here. She went out on the sidewalk and it was worse.

At first Brit couldn't see anything weird. The sky glowed a silvery gray with the city's ambient light; it was filled with low, slow-moving clouds—no! Those were the worms! She'd never seen them outside their tents before. What were they crawling on? Like ghosts in a movie they looked sort of see-through, rippling along what she could gradually make out as branch-like structures—and filmy-looking—leaves? Fainter than the worms themselves, the "leaves" shimmered in a way that made Brit's heart ache oddly, as if she was reading a sad love story.

What about that ticking noise, though, which she could hear all around now? It sounded tinier than the tiniest hail, and—she put her hands out to be certain—nothing was hitting her. Straining her eyes, Brit could finally see hundreds of miniscule white specks dropping from the worms. They bounced noiselessly off her skin and coat—and presumably her head—and clicked against the ground.

Experimentally she tried to crush some of them beneath her right Converse. Silence. Not even the soft scrape of a rubber sole on the cement. But when she lifted her foot she'd smashed the white specks beneath it to a powder, and an acrid smell wafted up to her from the pavement, like mildew. What—

On the street's other side a parked van lit up for a second as its door opened and shut. The brief light showed a navy coat; a long, pale ponytail; a round, pink face—Crofutt! He'd followed her somehow. Via those fireworks and sparklers he'd babbled about?

"Hey! This isn't a good place," he shouted across the road. "You really ought to come with me—"

Who cared how he'd found her? Brit ran back inside the building and slammed the door shut and locked it.

Crofutt kept shouting. "Dreams are dying back these days, and I think the reason for that's somewhere around here."

Her shoes were wetter than ever. And her socks. First chance she got—

"They're dying back. Something's killing them, something dangerous."

Dry socks and shoes. Clean underwear. She'd forgotten to—

"Are you listening? If you don't come out I'm going to call the cops."

"Go head!" Brit yelled back. What had he been raving about? Dreams dying back, like some kind of occult crop? "I've got a right to be here!" Well, she did, sort of—her parents had signed the mortgage papers yesterday. "What they gonna say 'bout you stalkin' a underage girl?"

That shut him up. Only for a moment.

"I'll call anonymously," Crofutt amended. "You shouldn't stay here. Not here."

An anonymous tip? How quickly would the cops respond? She might get away before they came.

And go where?

"At least tell me what you saw?" the man asked.

"What I—" She ought to stop answering him. It only encouraged him to keep talking.

"You were looking up. What did you see?"

Well, this was one person who would probably believe what she said.

Brit described the tents, the worms, the leaves and branches. The rain of specks. When she was done it was quiet again. Except for the ticking.

"That explains a lot." Crofutt wasn't shouting anymore. His voice felt close, like he was leaning on the door.

"Explain what?"

Crofutt had it all figured out. He called Brit a "Visioner," and said her power was translating the ways of "non-physical entities" into "concrete, manipulable analogies." It boiled down to her boiling down demons, angels—and other things, things without names, all the things most people couldn't see or understand—to simpler forms. The worms ate dreams—that was what the leaves were. The specks were their—excrement.

And so on. It was the nearest anyone had come to making sense, assuming she truly wasn't crazy. Brit felt completely willing to listen to Crofutt—through the door.

"Say you right," she finally half-admitted. "These worms eatin' up everybody's hopes an' dreams till ain't none left?"

"Pretty much. Then *they'll* vanish—leave, starve, however you lay out the concept. I've seen the effects of the cycle over and over—the '60s, the '80s—a lot of innocent people got hurt."

"I can look after myself okay," Brit assured him. Maybe he wasn't a creeper after all.

She still wasn't about to let him in, though. He could prove that another time, in the daylight, around other people.

And part of what he said didn't quite compute—"I can make these what you callin' 'entities' do like I want by how I see 'em?"

"Sort of. What they do also influences how they appear to you—"

"Awright. So what these worms turn into after they eat up everyone dreams? Some kinda gigantic moth?"

"Hmm. Could be."

Images of Japanese monster movies flitted in and out of Brit's head. She let them come and go. What she really needed to figure out was how to keep the worms from stripping all the silver dream leaves from people's thought vines—that was what she had decided to name the translucent branches curling through the night: thought vines. Which could belong to anybody. They were tangled up but there must be a way to trace them to their roots, to their sources, which could be anyone. Even her parents. Even her.

Wet and hungry and tired—that didn't matter. She had left home to find a way to convince Mom and Dad that she wasn't a whack job. That she knew what she was doing. Which meant she had to know it.

She stopped answering Mr. Crofutt's questions, and after a while he stopped asking them. She walked straight across the puddle to the stairway where her stuff was, not caring anymore how soaked she got. Because of the idea forming in her achy mind.

If the "entities" had to act like worms once she'd made them take that shape, they had to die like them. Die like worms.

She remembered from her sixth-grade science report how to kill tent caterpillars. You could cut down their nests and grind them to a pulp with heavy boots.

Brit didn't have boots that big. Nobody did.

You could burn them out.

Could the nests only she saw catch fire? And if they did would the flames spread and burn down her parents' building? Would the fire she set burn her to death?

She rolled up her sleeping bag and stuffed it in the pack. She pulled out her watch. Midnight. A long, long time till morning. Maybe she'd go home. Slog over to the Westin and find a cab. That'd be a laugh. She wouldn't have accomplished anything except to piss off Mom and Dad.

She wasn't scared. She climbed the rest of the way up and opened the door.

The roof was flat and covered in gravel. Brit scrunched over to the edge where the tent stuck up, betting it would be empty. Sure enough, the webbed walls were blank. No writhing. All the worms were out devouring dreams.

She took her box knife from her pants pocket and slashed at the nest's nearest side, but the knife sank in past its hilt and left no trace, while her hand wouldn't penetrate the webbing at all, not even a fraction of an inch. She remembered one of the rules for magic in the torn-up book of a runaway staying at their house: you should never use the same tools for mundane and spiritual tasks.

Brit cut things open with her box knife all the time. Mundane things. That left the cigar trimmer.

She hadn't really been going to give it to Dad. She got it out of the pack and the shop's bag: a pair of scissors with short, round blades. They made a nice, neat hole in the tent's side.

She pushed her head into the hole before she could think too much about what she was doing. It was awful anyway. She cut and cut and cut, past layers and layers of webs. Like squirming deeper and deeper inside a haunted house. Arms, shoulders, chest, stomach—she wanted to throw up. Here came that salty taste and the extra spit squirting into her mouth.

She wiggled back out again and breathed through her mouth, hard. And heard a siren in the street below. That was the goad she needed. She grabbed up her pack and went back in the tent. Completely.

The siren died away in the distance. So Crofutt hadn't turned her in after all. When she was sure they really weren't coming to get her she wiggled back out again. Drizzle had begun to fall while she shuddered and gagged inside; she actually thought about staying inside the nest all night.

But she had no guarantee the worms would stay out eating till sunrise.

Instead she sat cross-legged on the cold, damp gravel. She took out and unrolled the bag and half unzipped it so it lay like a puffy, down mantilla on her head and neck and shoulders, and formed a little shelter on either side of her. She laid out her tools underneath it: the butterfly lighter, the six fat cigars, ends ritually trimmed, ready to burn.

Then she waited for the worms' return. It wouldn't do any good to destroy an empty nest.

She tried not to sleep but dozed off despite the cold and discomfort. Obviously that meant she wasn't one bit scared of the morning. The red dawn. The horrible vibrations shaking the nest as its denizens poured back inside, ignoring—as she'd hoped they would—the slits and slices she'd made in their home.

Drawing on it as deeply as she could, Brit lit the first cigar. When it was going strong she reversed it and put the glowing end inside her mouth, bending to blow a stream of fragrant smoke into the nest's heart.

At first the worms stirred at the intrusion, blind heads seeking nonexistent fresh air, but by the fourth cigar they settled down where they were. To rest. The fifth. To sleep. The sixth. To loosen the grips of their hooked legs, fall to the tent's floor, and die.

She tossed the mantilla over the hole she'd used, changing it to a shroud.

Dizzy and nauseated, Brit struggled to her numb feet. Up, up, up: light and air and hope towered height upon height into heaven. The sun rose clear of a band of clouds. Too bright to the south and east to tell how many more nests awaited destruction.

She stumbled to the roof's other end. Her shadow stretched north across the city. Beyond it lay her parents and her home. Warmth. Blessed dryness. Anger, undoubtedly. But she would apologize. Even go to the psychiatrist a few times if that was what they wanted. She'd tell them that she'd been wrong, that they were right. That she wasn't scared anymore, because there had never been anything to be scared of.

She would tell them where she'd spent the night. And let them think they understood.

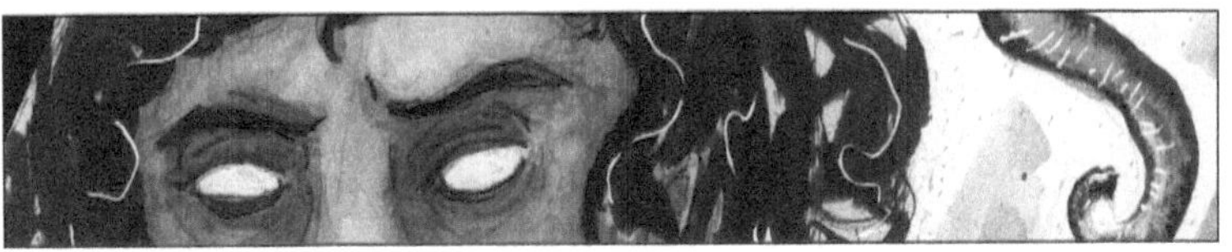

Street Worm: A Commentary

THIS REMARKABLE STORY INTRODUCES US TO BRIT (a spunky and gifted girl we will meet again in this collection in "Conversion Therapy"). She's a questioning young woman whose essential journey is discovering who she is as well as how to understand and manipulate her otherworldly visions. This story shows us Shawl's fabulous talent for crafting characters who are multi-layered, questioning, and powerful in ways that the world around them cannot comprehend. We see runaway Brit "passing" for different personalities as a means of survival, and using what other people assume about her as a way of conning them into helping her. Like many of Shawl's protagonists, the young woman exploits the weaknesses in the system to navigate it, and partners with those who are either empathetic or innocent victims of their situation.

The story gets hyperreal when it references Brit's supernatural skills as being akin to "The Shine" in Stephen King's *The Shining*, inviting readers to see the relationship between Crofutt and Brit as similar to Hallorann and Danny, inverted in race and gender. Crofutt helps Brit discover her power as a "visioner" who can "translate non-physical entities into concrete, manipulable analogies." This description treats her as a magical superhero type of *character* in the story proper, but we can also read it quite directly as a metaphor for the speculative fiction *writer*, for this is precisely what authors do with abstractions.

And what is Shawl doing with this story? Many things, especially in regard to cultural identity. Brit's independent spirit stands as a testimony to the autonomous power of young women who are *Othered* by their cultural circumstances. But the setting—the "street" of the title—makes this social allegory an interesting critique of the blindnesses of bourgeois life, as Brit hops in and out of fancy restaurants and abandoned buildings. Her encounters reveal the stratification of city life and the urban blight to which the dominant classes turn a blind eye. Brit uncovers the "worms" that are infested everywhere in the world, if one only pays attention. "The worms ate dreams," Brit realizes, coming to a clearer understanding of her vision. But here Shawl, the storyteller, *creates* dreams with her work, thereby calling attention to social issues, treating reality as allegory, and crafting a rich, culturally-informed drama.

—Michael Arnzen, PhD

Conversion Therapy

"THESE PEOPLE WON'T LET ME DO ANYTHING!" Delighta's artistic scrawl complained. "Including sleep—they keep waking me up all night to check I'm not dreamin about sex with other girls. They feed me rotten bananas and nasty peanut butter crackers for breakfast lunch and if I don't answer their questions right for dinner too." The rest of the lined and dirty page was torn away, leaving behind only random letters for Brit to guess into whole words.

She pulled the paper straighter, flatter, as if stretching it further would make the missing parts reappear. Of course not. She looked up at her friend and mentor, Mr. Crofutt, seated in her dorm room's sole chair. He nodded and frowned. "Looks like the trouble you picked up on is real," he said. She'd met him in Seattle two years ago, as a fourteen-year-old runaway. He was a counselor, freelance, and got her last summer's job at the arts camp he sometimes worked. The one where Brit gave in to the "bee" entities she was supposed to fight. The one where she'd used magic to lay occult claim to the nine kids she taught.

But arts camp had closed for the year and they'd scattered to their parents' homes. The one compensation Brit had received for letting go of her unofficially adopted charges was sensitivity to their whereabouts. Kids had to leave the nest, and Brit's nest wasn't even official—she'd only been the camp's martial arts instructor. Their parents came for them on the last day, but Brit had felt them near, had kept in touch all the following year via dreams and emails. And now—

"Where you find this?" Brit stood and went to the window. Nothing but trees outside.

"In the canoe, like I thought I would, from what you said. Easy enough to insist on a tour of the facilities; the camp director swallowed my 'concerned parent' cover story, and Grey and Tanzi are good actors."

And their parents trusted Mr. Crofutt, an established counselor in the community.

The window Brit looked out of faced east and north, away from Puget Sound. Toward Scrolls of Glory Purification and Rededication Camp, where Delighta Johnson was apparently being held against her thirteen-year-old will. Brit's worry over Delighta had soured her early matriculation into Evergreen College. The Ebonics she espoused to spite her *bougie* Mom and Dad hadn't fazed admissions. They knew brilliance when they saw it.

But Delighta—something was wrong with her. Brit could tell. Not only were they spiritual mother-and-child, they were both short and cursed with voices like Betty Boop. Both the fiercer because of that.

Soon as she moved in, Brit hung the folding fan Delighta had colored for her above her dorm room's doorway. She loved its rich colors—like a Summer of Love butterfly. But it only made her happy a few days. After trying a solid week to ignore the grinding unease she felt in her room and the extra jolt of queasiness she felt whenever she touched it walking in, Brit began trying to reach her favorite unofficial adoptee. When that didn't work she went on to contact all the other eight. It was Grey's cousin Jazman, Delighta's former crush, who tipped her the clue as to why Delighta hadn't answered Brit's calls and messages: she'd been sent away in disgrace. Incommunicado.

Brit broke out alternative methods then and finally got through. "Okay. I can communicate—a lil bit." Precision was not the strength of the bee-entity channels she'd employed. She'd persuaded the girl to write a letter about her abuse and leave it for Mr. Crofutt to collect. But the three fluttering scraps he and his supposed children had retrieved—only one of which bore anything like a coherent sentence—were not much help in terms of planning a rescue. And they'd be none at all in executing it.

Frustrated, Brit slapped the double-paned glass, flat-palmed. She could have broken it with an edge-strike, she was pretty sure. But what good would martial arts do? "We need us a map!"

"I could draw you a fair one from memory," Mr. Crofutt claimed. His supernatural power was Finding, and making maps was as easy for him as breathing in and out. Brit's power was called Visioning. She could make the invisible visible, make any non-physical magical entities she encountered physical so that they were vulnerable to physical attack. Like she'd done to create the giant tent worms the first time she met Mr. Crofutt. Like she'd done with the entities she turned into mystical bees last summer, when she took responsibility for Delighta and the rest of her class.

Problem was, doing anything about entities required a face-to-face confrontation. Besides, were entities even involved in this?

Grey and Tanzi swooped into the room, jangling the bells dangling from Brit's doorknob, fluttering the fan, laughing and drinking juice they'd bought from the hall's vending machine. They stopped after only a couple of steps. "What? Didn't we bring what you wanted?" Tanzi asked.

"You need us to go back?" Grey didn't wait for a response. "Cool. That place had a serious stench." At least that answered the entity question. If Grey smelled entities they were around the camp somewhere. Like Mr. Crofutt, the teen was shaping up to be another ace Finder.

"Yeah. Overnight if you can."

Mr. Crofutt grabbed his silver ponytail and put the fist holding it under his double chin. "I suppose I could make a sizeable donation to the church in exchange for a trial stay for my 'kids'. And there's a motel near the road into the camp for you and me, Brit."

"The donation gonna be funny money, I hope?"

"Oh, I'm cancelling that check soon as I issue it."

Brit kicked her heels in the Scrolls of Glory waiting room. Literally: her feet barely touched the carpet tiles beneath the padded stool where she sat. Scoot back far enough and her tai chi-slippered feet swung free. She hoped the ragged beat she drummed against its metal legs annoyed the woman keeping her waiting.

To be fair, on the phone the woman had clearly stated that they weren't actually looking for staff. Which made sense; the summer was practically over.

But the neck-pricking sensation of entities hovering over the adjacent property wouldn't allow Brit to wait calmly in the hotel for darkness and a chance to sneak onto the camp's grounds with Grey and Mr. Crofutt. She needed to be here *now*. Applying for a nonexistent job was the best excuse she could come up with for walking in here openly.

"Thanks for your patience. The Director is ready to see you," said the woman. No detectable signal had passed to her—no buzz of intercom or flash of light—but the woman sounded sure, and the door behind her opened. Sliding off the stool, Brit went in.

Peculiarly yellow dust motes filled the midafternoon sunlight slanting in at the office's windows. They gilded the spines of the books standing upright on the edge of his desk and smeared the frames of cross-stitched samplers lining the wall to Brit's left. She itched to wipe them clean. To her right ran a shelf holding more books—these stuffed with tasseled bookmarks and tattered, browning papers.

A slumping silhouette settled into the dark, high-backed chair behind the desk. From it came an entity vibe and a creaky voice. "Be seated, please." Brit perched on the edge of another stool. "An interesting application, Miss Williams."

"Ms."

Impossible to see the Director's expression with a row of wide, bright windows behind him, but he sounded more amused than angry. "As you wish. I suppose you refer to homosexuals as 'gays' as well. Or 'queers'." He laughed, a sound like crumpling a grocery bag. "What I wonder is how you expected to gain anything by filling out our form at the end of the season and then insisting on an interview. Invoking the Equal Employment Opportunity Commission is hardly going to . . . endear you to any prospective employer. So—" The door behind Brit opened—silently, but she felt the slight breeze of its movement dry the sudden sweat on her scalp. "—we suspected a trick."

Brit dropped to the musty carpet. Arms closed shut above her, where she'd just been—the receptionist—another entity. Rolling away and jumping upright she grabbed a book in each hand and ran toward the windows. *Smash!* Glass and wood scattered everywhere. Brit leapt through the jagged opening and landed on her feet, hardly stumbling. No one around to see. A quick glance and she oriented her bee-entity sense of the land with Mr. Crofutt's intel. Downhill lay the lake and boathouse and storage racks for a dozen canoes—full. Uphill lay the cabins. Dead ahead the commons: cafeteria probably empty but classrooms likely full of kids. Next to that the showers.

No time to launch a boat—and they'd only launch another after her. Brit ran for the nearest shelter—the showers—shoved the pine board door open on the cool darkness, the dampness—a scent of mildew rising like the echoing scuffs of her footsteps and a sniffling breath—No. No one should be in here but her.

But there again—a tiny, choking sob—

"Hello?"

"Mizz—Mizz Williams?" Spoken in mucous-clogged tones of disbelief.

"Delighta! What you doon alone and cryin in the dark? Where the light switch?"

"By the door where you are."

Brit reached and found it. "Why you ain't—" She stopped talking. The light flooding the cement walls and floor showed Delighta bound hand and foot, lying face down by the shower drain. Her short twists were mashed against the sides of her head, a sure sign she'd been fighting. White fuzz grew on the drain's grating and in a narrow circle around it, nearly touching the girl's tear-tracked cheek.

"Baby! What happen?" Brit made out extension cords hanging from towel hooks, clamps, gallon jugs, and a funnel on a wooden bench. She dragged the bench over to block the door; strange nobody had chased her here yet. Where was everyone? She went back to Delighta, sat her up, kissed her forehead, and began working on her knots.

"They—the counselors—they been tryin—"

Brit bit back the impulse to correct her charge's diction. If there was ever a time to relax her prohibition on her kids using AAVE the way she did, this was it.

"When other stuff didn't work they said maybe spendin time in here on my own would open my heart to the Glory."

The "Glory"? The rope was wet, the knots stubborn. Brit pulled a six-pointed shuriken from a secret pocket and began sawing. "What 'other stuff'?" She had an idea.

"Torture." Delighta's voice attempted matter-of-factness; a hurt quaver betrayed her. "Tellin me it's for my own good so I'll grow up straight; they give me shocks for lookin at naked girl pictures and enemas if they catch me play—*Ow*!"

"Sorry." Brit dropped the knife from her traitorously

trembling hand. She pulled loose the wet clothesline and exposed Delighta's wrists. "Only a scratch." She rubbed the girl's shallow cut; already the bleeding had basically stopped. Big exhale. Out with the shakes. In with the patience. She moved on to Delighta's ankles. The clothesline there glimmered in the gray light coming through the building's louvered vents. Not clothesline, but something thicker: clear plastic over a metallic core—the cable of a bike lock. Brit slashed at it in sudden frustration, blunting her blade, and Delighta jerked her legs back. Brit sighed and slouched forward, defeated. She would have to carry the girl to safety. She was strong enough. They'd be slow, though . . .

A scraping noise came from the wall standing at right angles to the door with the bench in front. From outside. Low. But the bench-stopped door didn't budge or even rattle. More scraping—higher? Climbing up the wall? Sliding over another bench, Brit used it to step onto a sink back and peer out of the vent at the wall's apex. She could barely see the ground; it teemed with ants—huge ants, big as throwing stars, though not absolutely-nuts sci-fi movie giants.

Visioning at work—Brit's secret power. She'd transformed the entities infesting Scrolls into ants, so now they'd be vulnerable. Though ants and bees were deadly enemies, anything that could kill ants could get rid of the entities.

She had come prepared. The other two times she'd Visioned entities, they came out insects also.

From a pocket—not a secret one, since nobody would think the contents mattered—she took a stick of ordinary-seeming chalk. Broke it in half. "Here." She handed part to Delighta. "Draw a line where the wall meets the floor, all aroun us."

"This is magic?" Delighta crawled to the far wall and began tracing a wide line at its base.

"Naw. You gonna find it in almost any hardware store. Boric acid." Not a pesticide but a repellent. Quickly, Brit finished laying down her sections of the chalk line and ran to reinforce the barrier at a few crucial spots with the last of her stub: the vents, the narrow space underneath the door, the white-circled drain. She checked for chinks in the cement where water pipes came in and sealed off five.

"There." The ant entities would stay away. For now. For long enough, Brit hoped, that Grey and Tanzi and Mr. Crofutt could find them and get them out of there. She examined the bike lock. With the help of icy water to reduce the swelling in the girl's feet and a few pumps of liquid soap for lubricant, they worked it off.

After that it was a mere matter of waiting. She cradled Delighta in her arms, leaned the girl against her legs, her knees up like mountains. All around them, all the rest of that soon-clouded afternoon, every wall scratched and scrabbled with the flood of questing entities.

Then, toward sunset, the flood receded. Ants were diurnal animals, Brit knew.

They had water. They had a place to pee and toilet paper. They had the power bar Brit brought to eat, but hunger persisted, and boredom combined with it almost irresistibly once Delighta finished her inflectionless recital of the tactics used to "purify" her of her emergent sexuality. So after only forty minutes of silence and a score of swift peeps out through the vents, Brit scooted the bench aside and opened the showers' door.

The surroundings were completely deserted. No sign of huge ants or humans. The commons a few feet away looked dark and empty, though this must be suppertime.

The original plan called for sneaking in to rescue Delighta tonight. Mr. Crofutt's final recon should be happening now. Where was he? Where were her kids Tanzi and Grey? Where was *anyone*?

Brit almost headed south, back to the offices she'd escaped earlier, to see who might be holed up there. But good sense prevailed and she shepherded her charge northward, to where a trailhead entered the forest's spreading shadows. The main road curved around the property's boundary to eventually hug the lakeshore, so they'd come to it if she could keep them on track, dead ahead. Over unfamiliar terrain. In the falling dusk.

Under the first of the alders Brit explained this strategy to Delighta, sounding confident. She reminded herself she had reason to: since last summer, when the bee entities transformed her, Brit no longer got lost.

The main path was broad. Distracting smaller branches coming off of it led nowhere important, so Brit hurried Delighta past them. Which was why they didn't find the first corpse till they'd been walking three quarters of a mile.

"I hafta pee," Delighta announced.

What could Brit say? They'd left the showers' toilets behind just minutes ago, but so what. She nodded toward the nearest side trail. "Go on. I be here."

Discreet rustling marked the girl's progress. Then: "*Ah! Aaah! Aaaa—*" Screams yanked Brit through tall weeds and brambles to where Delighta clutched her panties and pointed.

From the underside of a poplar's springy-looking limb hung one of the camp's five-inch ants, coated in what seemed like sunlit dust. Except there was no sun. A long spike protruded from its head, a sparkling ball stuck onto it like a weird Christmas ornament.

Brit knew what this was. *Ophiocordyceps unilateralis*. "Quiet," she said, and Delighta obeyed. For a wonder. She lectured into the silence. "That thing cain't hurt you. It dead."

At least part of it was. The part that threatened her and her swarm.

"Look." Brit picked a stick off the ground and knocked the ant's body down. The head stayed locked to the poplar limb by lifeless jaws. Delighta gave a tiny shriek followed by a nervous giggle.

"See? Dead." She kicked the crumbling chitin apart. "Now come on." They resumed their journey. Brit wished she could sing to stave off her worries, but someone searching might hear them.

But who? Who was chasing them? Who—or what—were the entities in control of Scrolls? The oversized enemy ants she'd first seen, or the fungus that appeared to be taking over the ants? Or both?

The next corpse settled that.

As twilight's dimness rose between bushes and tree trunks, smoke without fire, Brit found she guided Delighta more and more closely. She held Delighta's hand tight in her own, then wrapped an arm around the girl's tee-shirted shoulders. She told herself their mute caution would help them spot Mr. Crofutt and the others if the Finder came looking for them. That she was not really afraid.

She saw the man's dangling body ahead and covered Delighta's eyes. She clenched her teeth. She did not scream, or even grunt. Made no noise at all.

The bulging eyes and gaping mouth recalled the strange fruit of lynch mobs. But the gold powder dusting the dead man's skin was identical to the "sunlit" dust on the ant's corpse, and it tied their deaths together. The same danger had caused them: *Ophiocordyceps unilateralis*, aka Zombie Fungus. While studying the bees who were the template of the entities taking her over, Brit had delved into the biology of their natural rivals and frequent combatants, carpenter ants. And that of the *ants'* natural enemy, *O. unilateralis*, which apparently was in the process of enslaving and killing the camp's original entities. Her Visioning power had physicalized the first entities as ants, and the invaders as this fungus.

Zombie fungus. Which could attack both ants and other organisms. Such as human beings. Converting them to monsters. As it had apparently already done before Brit arrived. And now—probably this very afternoon—

"You known the Director? Mr. Scribner?"

"Ye-e-e-es . . . Mizz Brit, what's wrong?"

"Hope you didn't like him much. He dead too. Hangin up ahead in a tree we gotta go by."

"Dead? You mean like—"

"You be all right?"

"I guess."

They began to shuffle forward. In short glimpses as they passed, Brit saw how the Director's hands locked together around the branch he hung from. How the fingertips of his left dug too deeply into the wrist of his right. How the toes of his shoeless feet strained skyward, flexed hard in the same pain or ecstasy that threw back his head and opened his silent mouth. And though the true spore-bearing body would take days to develop, she thought she saw a soft, incipient bulge at the crown of his head . . .

So. Two entities. One the other's prey.

More indistinct shapes crowded the darkening treetops. Brit ignored them as well as she could and urged Delighta on. Finally, finally, they stumbled down into and back up out of a mucky ditch and there they were. The road. Impossibly civilized.

Which way to the motel? She checked the glowing geomagnetic grid underlying the world. South. They'd have to pass the camp's entrance. Maybe go off the shoulder on the opposite side.

A few feet beyond Scrolls' dirt-and-gravel turnoff, Mr. Crofutt's van sat, lights doused, motor running. "Stay here," Brit ordered Delighta, and ventured out of the horsetails and fireweed on her own.

Tanzi sat shotgun. Brit couldn't see anyone else.

Tanzi rolled down the window. "Hey! Grey and Mr. Crofutt found you?"

"Nope." She waved Delighta in. "We took the long way round."

Tanzi opened her door, smiling. "Lighta! I'm so glad you—but don't—don't cry!" She thumped Delighta awkwardly on her back as the girl climbed in over her.

"I'm not!" Wiping furiously at her lying eyes, Delighta shrugged off Tanzi's attempts at comforting her and flopped sideways on the back seat. "Let's blow."

"We gotta wait," Tanzi objected. "They'll be back soon—" Her voice thinned uncertainly.

"When?" Brit demanded. "They say?" She sat behind the wheel. "I got my learner's license. How about I drop you two at the motel an come back?"

Tanzi didn't know whether there'd be time. Brit decided not to push it. Fish-smelling mud caked her Spiras; she dug at the clumps on her left shoe with the toe of the right. Then cleaned the right with the left. Should she return to face the entities on her own? But the girls needed her protection. And she might miss the others.

Minutes passed. Full night reigned by the time Mr. Crofutt's white-and-purple clad paunch jounced into view. An old-fashioned flashlight illuminated it, pointed at the ground. Brit thought Grey must be invisible because he walked outside the bright circle. Then Mr. Crofutt switched the light off and got in alone. He shut the door. "Move over. I'm driving." He sounded gruff: sad or angry. He let out the brake and backed into the camp's entrance, but only to turn around and head the other way down the main road, toward the motel.

"Stop!" Brit lurched off the back bench and crouched between driver and passenger seats. "You gonna just leave? Where Grey?"

Mr. Crofutt kept going. "Time for the police. Grey's captured by the ants you Visioned up. They caught us outside a cabin." He leaned forward as if checking the left rearview mirror, then looked briefly over his shoulder at the empty road behind them. His enhanced eyesight—part of his Finder skill set—must have shown nothing to alarm him. He flipped on the van's headlights and sped up.

"You know for a fact the po-po wanna listen to you? Bout some little black kid foun trespassin on private property?"

"Well, you have a point, but yes. Since I'm white."

"Awright." Brit settled back into her seat. "We try it your way." She had to think what was best for her kids.

According to the motel rooms' "Welcome to Aberdeen County!" booklets, the closest police station was fifteen miles away. Too far. Mr. Crofutt agreed neighboring Copalis Crossing's Volunteer Fire Department was a better gamble. That was only three.

Filling the shallow tub for Tanzi and Delighta, Brit laid out the shirts she'd brought for them to sleep in. A tiny bottle of free shampoo dumped in under the faucet turned the water into a bubble bath. The girls squealed with pampered glee.

She loaded her jacket pockets with the rest of her power bars and hesitated, then turned on the TV. *Star Trek* reruns. "I'ma lock yall in, an you don't let nobody through that door cep me. Awright?"

Only one voice answered her. "Yes, Mizz Williams." That was Tanzi.

"Delighta?"

"She's holding her breath, Mizz—"

Brit rushed back in the bathroom. Half-obscured by hills of

white suds, Delighta lay flat on her back, six inches underwater. Eyes open, staring at nothing. Suiciding? "Out! Git out the tub!" Her fright startled Tanzi into jumping over the tub's rim.

"Delighta!" Arms plunged in to her elbows she hauled her adopted daughter free of the steaming bathwater. "Delighta!"

The girl blinked. Twice.

Brit turned to Tanzi, shivering and dripping on the bathroom floor. "Gimme a towel. Git one for yourself too." She pulled the plug to let the tub drain.

Dried off, Delighta seemed content to continue to stand naked and blank-faced. "You hear me?" Brit asked her. A slow nod. "You okay?" Another. "Why you so weird then?" No response. A hasty examination revealed nothing out of the ordinary except the cut on her wrist from Brit's shuriken, which was oddly pale. White, almost. Dead skin rendered transparent by soaking?

A knock on the motel room's front door roused Brit from her contemplation. Mr. Crofutt was ready for their return trip. "Comin!" she yelled. But what about Delighta—could Brit leave her here? Was that fair to Tanzi? She'd been unsure before, and now... With sudden decision she tugged a too-large glitter-printed tee over her damaged daughter's head.

"Put your clothes back on again, Tanzi." She yanked the covers from the nearest bed. "An carry this. You gonna spend the night in the back a Mr. Crofutt's van."

He led them down to the parking lot without one remark. Which was a good thing. Mr. Crofutt was the one who'd left Grey, who'd made this whole second trip necessary.

What a lie. It was all her fault.

She'd had no business adopting nine kids like that last summer. Barely not a kid herself anymore.

Copalis Crossing Fire Association shared building space with Aberdeen County Emergency Medical Services. Mr. Crofutt cut the van's engine and opened his door but then sat there.

"What we waitin for?" Brit asked.

"I called ahead. The dispatcher said somebody'd meet us." He gestured at the empty asphalt, the lightless windows. "Looks like we beat them."

Brit would have cursed if not for Tanzi and Delighta. "What kinda Deliverance—" Before she could finish, a blue-and-white squad car pulled in. Its human-looking driver and passenger glowed golden with dusty fungus spores. "Go! *Gogogogo!*"

Mr. Crofutt peeled out, door hanging open till he veered sharply enough to slam it shut. Zooming up Ocean Beach Road he shouted over the engine roar, "Entities?"

"Bad ones! Fungus infections—same as at Scrolls of Glory!"

The cop car was following them. Tanzi was visibly trying not to cry and having no luck. Delighta—Delighta craned over her seatback like she was ready for dessert and the cop car was made of ice cream. In its headlights a hungry gleam shone from her eyes.

"No siren," Mr. Crofutt observed. "You think they really are cops with no entities infecting them and—"

Whoop! Whoop! Whoopwhoop!

"Don't pull over! We're almost to the camp!"

The siren began undulating nonstop. Mr. Crofutt shook his head and slowed down, edging off the pavement.

"A little farther!" Brit begged.

"My reputation!" Mr. Crofutt objected—but he turned at the right intersection. The cop car gave up following them and sped ahead to park across the road.

"Stay in here!" Brit ordered the girls. The van was still—barely—rolling, but she got her door open and for the second time that day scrambled into and out of a weedy, mud-filled ditch. Running through the blinding white cones thrown by their car's headlights, she escaped the cop's roadblock. Headed for ants and more fungus. Shadowy trees surrounded her on three sides. On the fourth the openness of the camp's entrance drive beckoned.

But the cop car would come that way if Mr. Crofutt couldn't defeat either group of entities on his own. But the trees' shadows probably contained the same horrors she'd seen leaving—

A loudspeaker squawked, then blared recognizable words: "Come out with your hands up!" The squad car cruised into view. The driver steered with one hand and held a bullhorn in the other. He stopped and offered it to someone—some*thing*—riding beside him. "*Chik-lik-tikki-kik-kik-kichh!*" it shouted. From cabins and other buildings came the ominous sound of opening doors. Brit imagined giant ants and fungus-ridden kids and counselors pouring forth, spilling down the hillside to fight each other.

Before she saw them she saw Delighta. Barreling toward the cop car—with Mr. Crofutt and Tanzi right behind her. Delighta reached the car and opened its door and dragged out the driver. Brit couldn't see exactly what happened then—the car was in the way of most of it. Both fungus cop and girl landed on the ground, and only Delighta got up from it.

The near door—the one on the passenger side—burst open. The other entity tumbled out and scrabbled at the dirt. It began crawling away. Delighta fell on it from above.

Tanzi and Mr. Crofutt caught up. "Wait! Stop!" They grabbed Delighta by the shirt and tried to pull her off her victim. Brit ran to help, but before she arrived they succeeded. In the backwash of the car's headlights, Delighta's mouth shone gold and silver, as if smeared with metallic lip gloss.

The misshapen uniform lying on the shadowed earth seemed to move. It *was* moving: twisting and teeming like hot syrup in cold water. And the cop's face: ripples ran over it from opposite directions, crashed, receded...

"Get back!" Grey came down the hill surrounded by a crowd of ant entities. "You're not inoculated like me!" He flapped his arms. "Back!"

"What?" Brit and Tanzi edged away from the fallen cop. Delighta stood, turning her head in a slow, even arc as if scanning the cool night air. For something.

"The zombie fungus—the bad mind control entity?" Grey stopped just outside the headlights and gestured at the dozens of oversized ants. "The originals, the ants, started farming a—guess you'd call it an enemy? A different fungus that fights it."

Mr. Crofutt peered up from where he crouched over the shivering entity body. "So *that's* what I smell!" He straightened and pointed. "Strongest over that way, right?"

"Yeah. It needs a ton of water, so they picked the showers to incubate it in." Brit recalled the white ring around the floor drain by Delighta's face—her cut wrist—was that why she'd submerged herself in the bathtub? To irrigate her infection?

"So they your friends?" She caught Delighta in her arms, trapped the girl's head in her hands and forced it still. "Ants ain't want nothin from us bees but our honey. They kill us—"

"'Us bees'?" Grey's voice came now from the blackness where the other fungus cop had fallen. "I thought we were humans. With powers, sure, but look, ants—big ones like these even—they can sting us, eat our picnics I guess. That's all. It's the zombie fungus we've gotta be careful of, and once you've been inoculated with the one against it that the ants made—" He stood and stepped fully into the headlight beams, holding out arms glinting white to the elbows. "—and gave me? You're safe."

Brit looked at Mr. Crofutt. The enemy of my enemy is my friend? Was he buying that? "Listen. We come here to rescue my—my child." If Brit was a bee so was Delighta. So was Grey. So were all nine of the kids she'd claimed. "An that's what we gonna do! Tanzi! Come on! You too, Grey!" Shooing Tanzi ahead and dragging Delighta behind her she walked fast as she could up the driveway—till she saw the swarm of ants following them. Then she ran.

Easier this way than through the undergrowth.

She heard human feet behind her. But others too, and when she finally reached the van and she got her charges in and climbed in herself, she saw out of the windshield not only Grey and Mr. Crofutt in the middle of the shadow horde of ant entities gobbling up the ground. She saw the receptionist and another couple of vague, golden, adult-shaped outlines walking in their wake. Almost, it seemed, herding them.

Brit slammed the passenger side door shut, then lunged to lock the one on the driver's side. Delighta had the handle, trying to open it! "Git in the back," she yelled at Tanzi. "The way back." She fought Delighta and of course won—but why did the girl want out? The influence of the anti-zombie-fungus? "Delighta!"

Grey and Mr. Crofutt came up and pounded on the window. Didn't Mr. Crofutt have a key?

"I'll let them in my end," Tanzi announced from the rear, and before Brit could object she had opened half the double door past the last benches and covers and storage and Delighta, slick as tung oil, slipped out. And was running toward the attackers.

"Stop!" Brit shouted, pushing the door wider, shoving at Grey who was in the way! "Stop her!" she told Mr. Crofutt, but instead he stopped Brit! Caught and held her arms and *forced* her back into the van's interior. *Made* her sit. And saw her start to cry.

"Listen," he said. "Listen. Listen. *Listen. Listen!*"

"De-Delighta! Delighta's gone!" She forgot to use her "bad" English. "G-g-gone!"

"She'll be back! She'll be fine!" Mr. Crofutt eased up on the downward pressure and actually helped her stand. "Look at—oh, wait—I forgot you can't see as well as me in the dark. Let me—" Leading her around to the van's front end, he fished out his keys and stuck them in the ignition. "There." He snapped on the van's headlights.

Straining, Brit made out struggling figures where the camp's entrance drive met the road. The shorter ones—the kids were winning! Grey and Delighta rode the receptionist and the only other visible adult like playing piggyback. "Closer!" she commanded, throwing herself in the seat. She popped the parking brake off, cranked the key, and was reaching for the shift stick when Mr. Crofutt got in the other side.

"You ever drive a standard transmission before tonight?" he asked, swinging himself in place.

"My cousin Blaise's Beetle," she explained. "It a Volkswagen too." Though she drove as fast as she could change gears, by the time she got the car to the camp entrance the brief battle was as good as done. The ants swarmed over low, gradually deflating mounds. Whoever—whatever—their teeming shininess covered, it wasn't Grey or Delighta. Those two remained erect. Ignored, they straddled the rivers of insects streaming between their legs. White-coated arms on her hips, Delighta looked like a titanium oxide Colossus.

She looked nothing like a bee.

The ant entities made no move to attack her or Grey. Maybe when they "caught" him it hadn't been a hostile move, merely necessary for his inoculation?

Did Delighta still need to be rescued? Not if the zombie fungus was the entity to blame. Still—

Brit rolled down her window. "Let's go!" she shouted. Grey nudged Delighta and they came and got in. She turned around using the driveway, carefully avoiding crushing any ants.

The motel parking lot was mercifully empty and she had no trouble pulling in.

They weren't supposed to spend the night here, according to the original plan. Too easy for the entities to find them.

But dealing with Delighta's parents? Brit wanted to put that off as long as possible. She was muddy. Sweaty. Prickers in her hair. And so, so tired.

She gave the room key to Tanzi. Grey took one from Mr. Crofutt. She heard yelling and laughter as they went up the building's outdoors stairs. Three kids. Just kids.

And yet much more.

But what? What were they?

She asked Mr. Crofutt.

"I've been thinking about that," he said. "There used to be quite an array of skills. Besides me and my wife as Finders, and her brothers forming a pair of Visioners, my crew in Spokane had someone like Delighta could turn out to be—we called her a Pen. Like an EpiPen, though, not what you write with. She delivered . . . doses. She told us that in New York she'd worked with someone whose power was Charming—a man who lured the entities in. And there could be additional functions. Probably are. We only had five members.

"Counting me, now you have eleven."

Eleven. A family of eleven entity fighters. Though on good terms with certain entities themselves.

Tanzi's power hadn't even emerged yet.

Wearily, Brit opened the van's door, descended to the parking lot and set off for the stairs, wondering what wonders awaited her when she reached their top. And tomorrow.

Conversion Therapy: A Commentary

THE ORIGINAL CONTRIBUTION TO THIS anthology, "Conversion Therapy," is a return to Shawl's character Brit, who discovered her powers in "Street Worm" (and also subsequently appeared in a story named "Queen of Dirt," not included here) and here is using them for the benefit of others. She's become more in control of her abilities, achieved more of a sense of purpose and identity, and it's one that can be read as essentially *activist* in nature. The story structure is basically an escape from prison plot, and Shawl deftly handles the action and drama in this story through her skill for orchestrating rapidly-paced events. The tale is rife with choreographed battle sequences, but by having Brit rescue a character from a "conversion camp" for homosexuals, it becomes a kind of queer action adventure story.

Here we see Brit fully invested in her powers, subversively working with Crofutt while also doing her own independent thing, "knowing better" than the Father figure of the gang, in a quest to rescue Delighta from her oppressors. If "Street Worm" gave us worms as metaphors for blight, this story gives us ants, fantastically treating them as an analogy for compulsory normative heterosexuality. Even more stunning, they are spreading a "zombie fungus"—a metaphor for homophobic discourse and how it spreads and reproduces the ideology of hate. When Grey and Delighta and the others retaliate and destroy the ants in an epic battle scene we are not only witnessing a fantasy of avengement, but what might be read as a metaphoric youth movement. The young people take charge and deliver "doses" that suggest that today's young people—through assertive Charm and power alike—can inoculate culture against the heterosexually normative structures of the past.

—Michael Arnzen, PhD

Why Nisi Shawl Matters

by Michael Arnzen, PhD

I MET NISI SHAWL VERY BRIEFLY AT THE 2017 International Conference of the Fantastic in the Arts, during an awards banquet. We found each other during a break, talked swiftly about some of her amazing work, and I asked her a little bit about her longer stories, which I hadn't read. I was blown away by the imaginative scope of her projects, and intrigued by her experiments with ideas, mostly because they brought together concepts and cultures that others wouldn't dare, let alone have the capacity, to conceive. (A post-colonialist steampunk adventure set in the Congo involving King Leopold and Fabian Socialists? Only Shawl could dare a novel like *Everfair*). The award ceremony was about to begin, so I goofily asked if we could take a quick selfie together. Nisi seemed reluctant, because the occasion was so formal, and here she was stuck with a bearded white academic in a suit she barely knew who was acting like an adolescent fan with a cell phone. I think I said, "let's act like we're not having any fun here." Playfully, we both pulled our chins down and pouted, making a hilarious pair of long-faced frowns.

I look at that photo now and smile, not only because of the fond memory of her indulgence, but also because I feel like Nisi let her trickster self show through. Nisi is a bit of an intellectual trickster, playfully bringing together multiple genres in a way that challenges the reader's presumptions about just what it is they think they're reading... and I love that. I've come to see Nisi's writing as tricky, in all senses of that word, because it tends to make you reconsider what you assumed before you read it, and also *during* the reading of it. It educates and challenges you. It also, more than anything else, conjures a real sense of magic. And that's why Nisi Shawl matters: because she brings multi-culturalism to the table and explores speculative fiction as a means toward radically rethinking what it is that spec fic is and can be. And she conjures dreams through words like none other.

Her work in many ways is about the magic of belief—or the magic that belief can make anything possible, if we have a will to do it. Perhaps all good fantasy authors do this on some level, but Nisi Shawl courageously pushes her readers to think Otherwise, with a capital O, in a way that asks us to rethink our reality now; it is not just a mission that invites us to escape into some unproblematic SF utopia. She writes very consciously about reading and narrative and storytelling; not just to experiment with meta-fiction for its own sake, but to do so in the sense that invites us to consider different ways of knowing, whether by challenging the dominantly patriarchal meta-narratives that circulate invisibly in the genres she's working within, or by bringing a marginalized way of seeing to the fore, drawing from her experience and situation as an *intersectional* African-American woman writing speculative literature, fully awake about how power circulates across disparate communities.

Even that description—with identity marking labels like "African-American" or "woman" sounds too much like a box which I'm not comfortable using with Shawl, because—while she would totally and proudly own up to them—these are problematic labels where identities overlap, and Shawl should more appropriately be termed "intersectional" as she recognizes, represents, and writes from multiple subject positions that is complex, with overlapping issues at stake. Shawl once posted a roundtable discussion to *Locus magazine* (12 Jan 2012) about this very term, and her definition bears full citation here:

> . . . to my mind, "intersectionality" refers to the idea that one can relate to numerous sorts of marginalized identities, and that the effect of these marginalizations is synergistic—and needs to be seen as such. For instance, my identity includes my race, gender, age, physical disabilities, and so on. My experience as an African American is influenced by my gender, age, and physical ability, etc. So any analyses of the impact of racial factors on my life will be more accurate when they reflect these other factors as well.
>
> I think that intersectionality is modified not just by the experience of oppression, but also by the experience of privilege. So, again, my experience of my racial identity as an African American is transformed by my US citizenship, my high-functioning literacy, and so on.

Shawl's persistent inquiry into what makes one who they are—and her resistance to being pigeonholed by others—is not only one of her dominant questions as a thinker and educator, but also as an author, and her characters are persistently exploring identity, desire, and the limits that go with it.

A writer like Shawl, an Afrofuturist who is masterful at raising such issues, seduces the reader to question their own identity and how they either resist or play along with cultural belief systems that construct identity to begin with. I began this essay in first person, with a personal anecdote, because one of the issues that Shawl's writing immediately raises is what critics call the "situatedness" of one's interpretation. We all come to a text from a certain perspective, carrying a worldview that has been shaped by our situation in life, influenced by all the elements that Shawl raises in her definition of "intersectionality" above and more. When reading Nisi Shawl's work, one becomes hyperaware of their own circumstances in relation to the story, and how one's own cultural identity—riddled with assumptions about how stories should be told, how characters should act, how different elements are valued or seen as important—might lie beneath their interpretations of it.

Work like this asks you to recognize who you are, and who the author is as well, as it invokes a community of awareness as much as a fantasy of escape. So I should say right up front that I am more of a learner when I read Shawl's work than any kind of authority. But I think we all are, because she uses genre to teach us about various heritages and discourses that have been marginalized from most speculative fiction. (I'm also one of probably only a handful of white male academics who has taken a course called "African-American Lesbian Poets of the 1970s," and perhaps part of an even smaller group of horror authors who have also studied and written Marxist-Feminist literary criticism, so I still feel my thoughts about her writing are informed, even if far less so than, say, a black literary scholar—and I also know that Shawl's work is more inclusive than exclusive, so enough conditionalizing!). No matter who you are, or what your situation is in our culture—which thank goodness is growing in self-awareness thanks to writers like Shawl—if you are new to this author's wild fiction, you will learn a lot from this volume. And it's about time.

Shawl too is situated, and it is useful to be aware of the various conflicting identities she embodies and works through in her writing. She is an African-American woman writer, identifying as bi-sexual, highly educated and working in a genre that has been dominated by heterosexual white male writers and readers alike perhaps since its popularization ... and she brings the politics of this situation to the table in her stories. She is an informed, activist writer, but also sees the activism inherent to the genre as a tool for social progress. Mostly, in my opinion, she invites us to want to change the encrusted tropes of the genre by thinking about alternative possibilities, and this is why speculative fiction—science fiction, fantasy, and horror—is her domain.

If science fiction is a possibility space, a place for wondering "what might be," then Nisi Shawl's imagination provides alternative ways of exploring this space all while looking around the corners and edges and *fearlessly* getting us to reconsider those, too. She writes about threats and fears and anxieties the way the best horror writers do—as subjective experiences—and her work is rife with ghosts, mythological beings, supernatural powers, voodoo, and black magic. But I do not think of her as a horror writer, *per se*, let alone a writer limited by any one genre. She seems very distrustful of boundary lines, and that's a good thing. Instead, I think of her as a fearless fabulist, doing whatever she likes across the genres that allow for free imaginative reinvention. In Shawl's work the supernatural realm and the world of magic is treated as a *natural* location for setting, but she also shows how writers can explore genres of unreality in new ways in order to *resist naturalizing tendencies* as they get encrusted in a genre.

Part of Shawl's magic is accomplished through genre hybridization, drawing from radically different areas of research and trope alike—mixing, say, Nigerian folklore with contemporary fantasy and adding in a dash of action-adventure—in a way that fascinates the reader and educates them at the same time. It invites openness and inquiry, as everyone in her stories is always unsettled, unmoored, unattached to the safety of *status quo* (save for the villains, who all seem threatened and motivated only by a conservative impulse to keep things "safe" for themselves) . . . and yet these "outsider" characters—for the most part women—are also at the same time connected to their communities, motivated by love and acceptance, faithful to their heritage and families, growing into their power in their own way, and always, *always*, strong.

Critiquing culture by writing in such a self-aware manner, playing with stock genre tropes that threaten to rewrite the very rules by which we understand a genre, is courageous writing. Nisi Shawl writes about characters that some readers may not immediately identify with and she does not play it safe. A genre trickster, Shawl doesn't just jump into the driver's seat of a car she's been given by her predecessors in the genre and step on the gas. She first gets under the engine and *tricks it out* and makes it her own vehicle first. Sure, she openly acknowledges her diverse influences—which are many and varied—but even in this small sampling of her work collected here, you will see they range from Stephen King novels to African folklore to the nightly news. She's been doing this kind of intersectional remixing for quite a while, rising to acclaim in the speculative fiction community, winning awards like the Tiptree (in 2008 for her collection *Filter House*) to editing important anthologies like *Strange Matings* (2015) to running educational programs about acknowledging and appreciating diversity in courses and workshops like *Writing the Other* (a mini-textbook that every creative writer should read).

But I think you'd know all this and recognize you were reading an African-American woman's writing even if you picked up this book and didn't know anything about Shawl, perhaps foremost because her primary characters are often young African-American women—a demographic largely under-represented in SF/F throughout the 20th Century except as latently racist/sexist stereotypes. But it isn't just the *presence* of these characters—who often aren't normatively sexual either—that makes Shawl's fiction so compelling and important. It's the way these character's stories are about power, even as they might be struggling to learn it or master it while navigating a thorny world of cultural difference.

And sometimes, using the strategies of SF/F, Shawl—while drawing from historical reality—remakes the world into something altogether unique, "keeping it real" precisely by playing with the unrealities of the fantastic. Her stories teach us to read Otherwise. And they validate the experience and heritage of readers who haven't seen their own perspectives and cultural situations represented in the genre. Her writing brings a spotlight to the secret places where people's lives overlap, with unspoken or uneasy conflicts and also intersecting commonalities. And this is why Nisi Shawl matters.

If you still don't get it, I have a photo to show you. It's of us playfully frowning. Get over yourself and try again.

In Conversation with Nisi Shawl

Eric J. Guignard: Hi Nisi, and great to chat with you here. Thanks so much for your time and for being part of this project! I've always been fascinated by mythology origin stories, imagining how a world or people or idea began or, perhaps, *is* beginning. This is something you've explored often in your stories, in perceptive and whimsical ways, such as in "At the Huts of Ajala," "Wonder-Worker-of-the-World," and "Down in the Flood," amongst others. Does this tie into a love of folklore or any particular mythology, or perhaps an homage to the forms, or is it more an enjoyment simply to birth new worlds and parables?

Nisi Shawl: Myths are collective truths that may or may not be fact-based. That's also what I write: truths. So always I'm trying to present readers with myths, though sometimes these look more like myths' traditional presentations and sometimes less. Sometimes they're more easily recognized as shared stories. Sometimes they're stories that I hope will eventually become widely shared, claimed by community.

The three titles you mention in your question were all deliberately drawing on different bodies of mythology. "Ajala" came out of an assignment from my godmother, Luisah Teish, to write about how I came to choose my head before I was born, and it owes much of its terminology and action to the Ifa cosmology of the Yoruba-speaking people of West Africa. "Wonder-Worker" was my attempt to Africanize a recurrent theme in Christian and pre-Christian myth from around the world. There are many, many European fairy tales, for instance, in which a woman becomes the bride of a supernatural being and must keep his house according to seemingly arbitrary rules. In "Flood" I wanted to reclaim the Mediterranean goddess Tiamat and frame her defeat by her son as victory. Changing our perspective on a particular myth is a powerful tool for changing the aspect of the world depicted in that myth. Changing Tiamat's defeat into victory is my way of overthrowing patriarchy.

EJG: I adore your dark fantasy story, "The Beads of Ku," relating Fulla Fulla's life and the turns and decisions that lead her to eventually barter in the Marketplace of Death. There are themes of family (motherhood and marriage), magic, and power shifts woven throughout. It's sweet, although ultimately tragic, a cautionary tale on many levels. I feel that often your characters have unexpectedly triumphant endings in your stories, though always, seemingly, in unanticipated ways, and at a cost. Here, Fulla Fulla tricked the King of Death to save her husband, but it left her trapped behind. In another story, "Cruel Sistah," Dory manages to finger her own murderer from beyond the grave through ghostly music, which leads to the murderer's suicide. In "The Tawny Bitch," Belle manages to escape her captors with help of a spectral dog, but after all she was forced to endure . . . Is this something you believe or have undergone in life, that people must first endure great hardships in order to be propelled forward or to achieve greatness? Do you have this idea in mind when writing the end of a story, or is it more an instinctive response to conflict resolution in storytelling?

NS: First, I'll say that writing stories involving unanticipated events is pretty much my job as an author. If you know what's going to happen in a story, why bother reading it? Second, though, I've recently been editing an anthology of speculative fiction by people of color, and I've seen the sort of "high cost victory" complex you're talking about here over and over. And it has also been noted in the works of Octavia E. Butler. My take is that having a history—personal and cultural—of paying high prices for survival lends itself to mirroring that circumstance in our fiction.

EJG: What do you love most about the writing process?

NS: Ahh. I love that feeling when I *get it right*, when the word I want or the scene I'm striving to depict comes through. I love also the feeling of discovery, when I'm writing something on trust, without understanding how it's going to work or why—and then it *does*, it makes sense, it's exactly what's needed. And I love when a reader affirms I've succeeded, when they get my joke or pick up my reference or understand more than I have flat-out stated on the page. Those are the moments. Those are the feelings.

EJG: You've been on the forefront of a number of works involved with Afrofuturism (particularly through your novel *Everfair* and your anthology *Strange Matings*), which, as an aesthetic, explores or reimagines science fiction, history, magic realism, mythology, technology, and culture (amongst other socio-political ideals and art forms), from an African viewpoint. Afrofuturism is considered a relatively new movement, with the term coined in 1993 by Mark Dery in his essay, "Black to the Future," although the artistic philosophy has roots going further back to the 1950s emerging through the music and poetry of pioneerist, Sun Ra, and even beyond that to the writings of author Martin R. Delany.

Particularly with the immense success of this year's movie, *Black Panther*, there has been a growing visibility and attraction to Afrofuturism. What do you think the future holds for this movement, in terms of both creativity and in ideology?

NS: We'll see what's to come, won't we? White critic Mark Dery invented the term Afrofuturism in connection with an interview he conducted with Samuel R. Delany. Since then, we African-descended people have wrestled with defining it for ourselves. Nnedi Okorafor pointed out that just examining the question in terms of demographics, the large number of African-descended people living in African countries should make them a majority in the movement. But the reality is that Afrofuturism as a mode of creativity is dominated by North Americans, and especially by USians such as myself. In the absence of a coherent ideology, all we can do is work with it, dance with it, play with it. That's what I'm doing when I call *Everfair* a novel of AfroRetroFuturism. "Retrofuturism" is a term steampunks apply to their way of re-envisioning the past with the inclusion of future technologies—and vice versa. Combining that with an Afrocentric viewpoint is very much my intent with *Everfair* and related stories. Perhaps that's what's next? Mashups?

EJG: With co-author Cynthia Ward, you published the non-fiction manual, *Writing the Other: A Practical Approach*, which is now considered "the standard text on diverse character representation in the imaginative genres." I understand this project grew out of a Clarion West Writers Workshop in 1992, and over the course of thirteen years you published papers on the subject, taught workshops, and developed exercises and techniques before compiling the material into the book in 2005. Since now it is thirteen *more* years since its publication, do you find attitudes about this subject have improved, or that authors are more willing to take knowledgeable attempts at writing outside the lives they are familiar with? What are some newer insights you may have gleaned, or advice to offer, given today's climate of genre writers?

NS: My co-author Cynthia Ward and I are currently in the midst of figuring out what to do in terms of a putting together a new edition of *Writing the Other*, with the help of K. Tempest Bradford. Tempest has been instrumental in making WtO classes and workshops more widely available via the internet; her input is going to be essential.

In terms of ROAARS traits (demographic traits considered important in classifying people), two have risen in how important they're considered: citizenship, and the differentiation between trans and cis in gender identity ("cis" means in agreement with gender assigned at birth; "trans" means in agreement with another identity). These types of categorizations need to be dealt with in our new edition. We may also want to delve deeper into North America's persistent denial of class as an important demographic marker.

EJG: What other authors do you read to inspire you to continually write such smart, diverse, dark, and fantastic types of fiction?

NS: Thank you for your kind words! I read mostly for work, these days—I have very little choice in what I read, actually, because whatever it is I'm going to have to write about it or critique it or review it when I'm done. Generally speaking, reviews must cover newer books. My series on the history of black science fiction for Tor.com is an exception. But I'm actually re-reading those books and short stories, so I don't know if those titles count as answers to your question.

I do read a ton of Samuel R. Delany, whenever I can. His understanding of language—what it can do, how it can do it—is supreme. A good translation of the French author Colette is literary lusciousness. Tanith Lee's fantasies have hit my sweet spot several times. New writer Kai Ashante Wilson's work bathes me in continual ecstasy. C.J. Cherryh's science fiction grips me, fascinates me, makes me think and feel like an alien. Gwyneth Jones keeps questioning hidden assumptions with audacity and vigor and power and joy. John Crowley, Nick Harkaway, Nalo Hopkinson, L. Timmel Duchamp, Chris N. Brown, Matt Ruff, Malka Older—how many pages do you want me to take?

EJG: All great authors to follow! Now, I'm really excited to be able to include in this primer a new short story from you that continues the series of Brit Williams, the teenage protagonist who discovers she has a unique supernatural power, and her subsequent years learning to use that power to help others like herself and to defeat malevolent "entities." I also included in this book the first story in the series, "Street Worm," and although not also included, I did enjoy the second story in the series, "Queen of Dirt" very much. You've developed a world where magic exists in a select few, and which is as rich as any other superhero who finds him/herself struggling to maintain normalcy while also saving the world. These stories are thrilling and thoughtful, with themes of individuality, discovery of self, loyalty, and love, as well as noteworthy side stories of rebellion against sexual indoctrination and Brit's choice to speak African American Vernacular English (AAVE, or "Ebonics"), even when she is highly literate and articulate. I understand you've also written more of Brit previously as a secondary character in an unpublished novel, but this storyline just seems ripe to expand into YA mystery/ thriller novels. What was the genesis of Brit's creation, and what lies ahead for her? Do you have ideas hopes for her character already, or do you prefer to let her "write her own journey"?

NS: Originally, Brit was the best friend of Iyata, the main character of my unpublished YA novel *Verdé*. As of this writing I've begun sending chapters of *Verdé* to my Patreon supporters. In the novel, Brit is a bit older than Iyata and has been "double-promoted" out of their shared high-school to college. So that's set very soon after "Conversion Therapy," the story you've included here. I've always anticipated writing a novel focused mainly on Brit and her further adventures, and I hope I do get to some day.

EJG: You have worked a wide array of non-writing jobs, such as janitor, cook, structural steel sales rep, musician, au pair, artists' model, etc. Knowing that sometimes we take jobs out of necessity rather than by preference, presumably the variety of life experiences engaged in diverse vocations can at least be used as fodder for new or unexpected ideas. Would you consider it has been beneficial to your growth as a writer by experiencing such varied occupations, or has it seemed it's just detracted from writing-centric endeavors?

NS: I made a conscious decision early on not to take jobs that competed with writing for my time and attention. Interesting jobs that required creativity were out. On the other hand, as you note, a variety of experiences can help in the quest for verisimilitude. So yes, I had to work. And I had to accept positions that not only paid me money but did little to interfere with my calling. But it worked out, in the end.

My last full-time day job ended seventeen years ago. Since then I've been able to make a living with my writing and writing-related work: teaching, editing, and so on. I have had a great deal of help doing that. I'm very, very lucky.

EJG: What's something that people think they know about you or your writing, that isn't true?

NS: *Hmm.* Thus far no one has told me anything about me or my writing I'd say was a lie. If it's true for them, it's true in at least that particular way.

EJG: What does the future hold for Nisi Shawl's writing career?

NS: I have no control over that! I have plans—I've sold a middle grade historical fantasy, *Speculation*, which will appear in Fall, 2019 from Lee and Low. The aforementioned anthology of original speculative fiction by People of Color, *New Suns*, will appear in Spring, 2019 from Solaris. Somehow *Kinning*, my sequel to *Everfair*, is going to come out. I promise. I hope.

But really? There's no telling. I'm just going to breathe. Keep an open mind. As hip hop artist Suga Free sang way back in 1997, "If you stay ready, you ain't got to get ready."

EJG: Thanks Nisi, and I know many readers will be eagerly awaiting all your latest forthcoming books. Wishing the best of success for each of them!

(May 2, 2018)

Written On The Water: An Essay

by Nisi Shawl

OUR MINDS ARE MALLEABLE, OUR MEMORIES FLUID. Do you recall the first instance of your engagement with the literature of the fantastic? For most of us that moment occurred too early to be easily recoverable—fairy tales told as we fell asleep, cartoons, films, puppet shows. What about your first engagement with science fiction? For some that instance came at a time more choate. Take a moment to remember it if you can.

My first verifiable encounter with a science fiction text was with a juvenile book called *Space Cat* by Ruthven Todd. Paul Galdone was the illustrator. I say verifiable because this book does exist, though I don't own a copy. You can buy one on eBay, along with others in the series, including *Space Cat Meets Mars* and *Space Cat and the Kittens*. Todd was a Scot and a conscientious objector, but that probably didn't figure into my enjoyment of this story of a cat clawing up jewels from the rubbery surface of the moon. Or perhaps it did, but without my conscious knowledge.

Another book—*Tatsinda*, by Elizabeth Enright, illustrated by Irene Haas—came into my life later, but has had as big an influence. It is one of those stories I reflect on frequently and use as a benchmarks for others. All of us who care about such things have an inventory of what are sometimes referred to as sacred texts: those we prize because of how powerfully they have affected us. Those we hold dear. Nowadays I'd classify *Tatsinda* as a "Lost Race" narrative, part of a subgenre peculiar to Victorian literature. Usually these narratives are set in the homelands of people of color at a moment just prior to, or during, their colonization—Africa, South America, Australia—and involve a white explorer discovering the decadent remnants of a white civilization in the midst of nonwhite savages. But in *Tatsinda* the white race is located in an even whiter wilderness at the North Pole ("the top of the world," Enright calls it), and the interloper is a slightly-less-white girl. I didn't know how iconoclastic this take on the Lost Race narrative was at the time, but my mind and heart found great comfort in descriptions of Tatsinda's brown eyes and golden hair as contrasted with the Lost Race's blue eyes and "glittering white hair like snow crystals."

As you can probably tell by the quotes, I *do* own a copy of *Tatsinda*. I've reread it several times over the last twenty years. Reread it with changed eyes, a changed heart. My mind being malleable, my needs have changed, those I now bring to the book. So of course I come away from it now with new and different sorts of satisfaction than those I found in my encounters with it at the school library as an eight-year-old.

As a child of nine and ten I was a fan of Burroughs's *Tarzan* novels. I somehow managed to make of my imaginal self an adult white Englishman, far superior to the ooga-booga blacks I impressed with my strength and rationality. At this point Burroughs's *Tarzan* books are as good as unreadable to me—the closest I can come to them is Pat Murphy's *Wild Angel*, the tale of a feral child of the California Gold Rush named Sarah McKensie who is raised by wolves.

The character of Sarah is a much better fit with the identity I've established and accepted for myself. It's not so much that I carry a model of my identity about with me as I read so I can match a book's characters against it. No. The process feels more to me as though I use my identity model as a mode of transportation, a way of traveling through the story. I become a Nisi Engine, tracing a track the book's author has laid out for me. The track often winds through the mental and emotional interiors of a story's characters, and often it leads me into mimicking their actions. You might say my imaginal self peers out at the story through eyeholes that pierce these characters' heads, experiences the story by the grace of their senses. I'm an infiltrator. I'm an echo. The closer the resemblance between my model of my identity and the character being evoked, the truer the echo, the more seamless my infiltration. And since adolescence it has become extremely difficult for me to array my identity model in a Lord Greystoke suit. Though the Tarzan texts remain essentially the same, they are for the moment inaccessible to me because of this. The mind on which I rewrite them as I reread them has become an incompatible medium, rejecting their inks.

In the case of *The Enchanted Castle* by E. Nesbit, a Fabian Socialist and a famous Victorian children's author, the text itself has changed. Or actually, it had been previously changed, and as an adult I have discovered the original. With its racism intact: When one young hero named Gerald applies boot polish to his hands and face to pose as an Indian conjurer at a fair, his brother declares that he looks "just like a nigger!" I'm quite sure that even in fifth grade I would have recognized name-calling of that nature as unacceptable, and been thrown completely out of the book. So though I no longer have a copy of a Bowdlerized edition, I'm sure that's what I first read. I was taught not to forgive that taunt, and I doubt I would have, even in so indirect an application, even if it meant foregoing the pleasures of *The Enchanted Castle*. And the pleasures are considerable; it's my favorite book by Nesbit, who is one of my very favorite authors, and I find it at once hopeful, disturbing, and elegiac. Still.

These are some of my sacred texts, sacred in the sense that I hold them dear.

Sacredness has another definition, too, a more strictly religious one. I practice a religious tradition based in West Africa and known as Ifa, and we have a sacred text to which we refer when doing divination. It, too, is known as Ifa. A text that is sacred can also be called "canonical," and this word carries connotations of orthodoxy and definitiveness. Canonical texts are conceived of as finished, as complete and unchanging, but in this sense Ifa is non-canonical in its very sacredness, because the Ifa text is constantly being revised based on the observations of those invoking it via divination.

Ifa is composed of 256 *odu* (literally "vessels") containing thousands of verses. To the verses passed down from generations of diviners in Yorubaphone Africa and the lands of its diaspora are appended contemporary commentaries; these commentaries include the names of those divining and of those posing the questions divined upon, as well as interpretations and applications of the verses referred to and their results. Thus one who practices Ifa transforms a holy text by that practice. What is sacred changes. And it does so through a sacred process.

In Octavia E. Butler's *Parable of the Sower*, her heroine Lauren Oya Olamina declares:

"The only lasting truth
is change.
God
is change."

Olamina creates this text and others as part of a religion called Earthseed; this manufactured religion is the social tool with which she intends to help the human race leave planet Earth. Cynical though this view is in the way it sees religion as a means to an end rather than as an end in itself, the Earthseed religion did attract sincere followers in the world of the Parable books—and it has done so in our world, also. This is because Earthseed is full of compelling concepts, among them the equation of the sacred with change. Change is inevitable, and ineffable. It is omnipresent, inescapable. It occupies the core of my periodic return to my sacred texts.

I change. The world around me changes. I reread my sacred texts to learn how they have changed in response to my changes or those of the world—changes in actuality, or in interpretation or emphasis, or all of the above.

Rereading is always, to me, rewriting. As I reread the texts I love, those that are dear to me, their words spill away from me into new meanings, filling up the fresh impressions I have left on the world by making my way through it. The hollow places and questions and emptinesses I have come upon in my continuing explorations open to receive thoughts that were always waiting to occur.

Heraclitus, an ancient philosopher, is famous for saying no one can ever step in the same river twice. Can you read the same story twice? Not if it's a sacred one—though you may reread the book containing that story four or five times. If it's sacred, it's alive. If it's alive, it changes. It is written on the water, and water flows.

I can never again read *Tatsinda* for the first time. Or the third time, the fifth, the eighth. But each iteration has its own beauty, its own strength. Most recently I read it aloud with a (now ex-) lover, who scorned it as a mere child's tale, who deliberately mispronounced its neologisms and mocked its improbable bestiary. None of his dissing made me cherish the book less; I only added a level of defenses between that man and the part of me that keeps returning to Tatsinda's realm, Tatrajan, to find there the old and new, the familiar and unexpected.

In my rereadings of *The Enchanted Castle* I often run into earlier models of myself. The memories it evokes are a potent element of the book's charm: memories of the marble-floored rooms where I first immersed myself in it, and the way I equated those rooms' coolness with the secret spaces within living sculptures of dinosaurs, where the story's heroes hid themselves; memories of imitating the roofless-mouthed speech of the Ugli-Wuglis, hilarious and horrible at the same time. The *Space Cat* books remind me of our family's orange tabby, Archibald Fitzrowr the Third, who I quite naturally conflated with Todd's feline adventurer Flyball. These are memories of earlier encounters, but they did not exist at the time of those earlier encounters. Though they reference them, these memories belong to later visits to my sacred texts, later versions of them.

My knowledge of the racist epithet version of *The Enchanted Castle* did not exist until my rereading of it, either. I add that understanding to my relationship with this story and the relationship changes. That change is not an end.

When will I be able to reread—and thus rewrite—*Tarzan*? I do need to reclaim his crocodile-dispatching knife, those mighty thews, the majestic solitude of his treetop fortress in the depths of a viridian darkness. Would an ability to radically alter my identity model help? Or ought I to try another strategy? I may attempt to add a bit more insulation between my identity and the character of Lord Greystoke—insulation such as the firm intention of filling that awkward gap with another novel, one all my own.

Holding onto an intention such as that I'll be able to dig new courses for the stories of *Tarzan* to run through. I'll break down dams. The books' meanings will be transformed, becoming sacred once again.

A Bibliography of English Language Fiction for Nisi Shawl

FOLLOWING IS A COMPLETE BIBLIOGRAPHY OF ENGLISH language fiction for Nisi Shawl through December, 2018. Not included are: foreign language translations, individual pieces of non-fiction, or individual pieces of poetry.

Abbreviations Used:

(1) = indicates story's first publication. Omitted if story first published in author collection.
(c) = indicates the collection containing this story. If the collection is listed first, the story's first appearance was in this collection.
(r) = indicates this is a reprint appearance.
anth. = anthology
mag. = magazine
f.c. = fiction collection
ed. = edited
v. = magazine volume number
# = magazine issue number

SHORT FICTION

"**A**t the Huts of Ajala"

(1) *Dark Matter: A Century of Speculative Fiction from the African Diaspora* (anth., ed. Sheree R. Thomas): Aspect/ Warner Books, 2000.

(c) *Filter House* (f.c.): Aqueduct Press, 2008.

(c) *Exploring Dark Short Fiction #3: A Primer to Nisi Shawl* (f.c., ed. Eric J. Guignard): Dark Moon Books, 2018.

"An **A**wfully Big Adventure"

(1) *An Alphabet of Embers: An Anthology of Unclassifiables* (anth., ed. Rose Lemberg): Stone Bird Press, 2016.

(r) *Fantastic Stories of the Imagination* (e-mag., #357): Wilder Publications, Nov./Dec. 2016.

"The **B**eads of Ku"

(1) *Rosebud* (mag., #23): Rosebud, Inc., Apr. 2002.

(c) *Filter House* (f.c.): Aqueduct Press, 2008.

(c) *Exploring Dark Short Fiction #3: A Primer to Nisi Shawl* (f.c., ed. Eric J. Guignard): Dark Moon Books, 2018.

"A **B**eautiful Stream"

(1) *Cranky Ladies of History* (anth., ed. Tansy Rayner Roberts and Tehani Wessely): FableCroft Publishing, 2015.

"**B**eyond the Lighthouse"

(1) *River* (anth., ed. Alma Alexander): Dark Quest Books, 2011.

"**B**ird Day"

(c) *Filter House* (f.c.): Aqueduct Press, 2008.

(r) *Alas!* (online media): amptoons.com, Dec. 2009.

"**B**lack Betty"

(1) *Crossed Genres* (mag., #36): Crossed Genres Publications, Dec. 2011.

(r) *LeVar Burton Reads* (podcast/ audio): Stitcher., Jun. 2018.

"But She's Only a Dream"

(1) *Trabuco Road* (e-mag., #3): Trabuco Road, Mar. 2007.

(r) *Unconventional Fantasy: A Celebration of Forty Years of the World Fantasy Convention* (anth., ed. Peggy Rae Sapienza, Jean Marie Ward, Bill Campbell, and Sam Lubell): Baltimore Washington Area Worldcon Association, Inc., 2014.

(c) *Filter House* (f.c.): Aqueduct Press, 2008.

"The Colors of Money"

(1) *Sunvault: Stories of Solarpunk and Eco-Speculation* (anth., ed. Phoebe Wagner and Brontë Christopher Wieland): Upper Rubber Boot Books, 2017.

"Cruel Sistah"

(1) *Asimov's Science Fiction* (mag., v.29, #10/11): Dell Magazines, Oct./Nov. 2005.

(r) *The Year's Best Fantasy and Horror: Nineteenth Annual Collection* (anth., ed. Ellen Datlow, Kelly Link, and Gavin J. Grant): St. Martin's Griffin, 2006.

(r) *Ghosts: Recent Hauntings* (anth., ed. Paula Guran): Prime Books, 2012.

(r) *Nightmare Magazine* (online media): nightmare-mag.com, Oct. 2016.

"Deep End"

(1) *So Long Been Dreaming: Postcolonial Science Fiction & Fantasy* (anth., ed. Uppinder Mehan and Nalo Hopkinson): Arsenal Pulp Press, 2004.

(r) *2007 Think GalactiCon Discussion Primer* (chapbook): Think GalactiCon, 2007.

(r) *Lightspeed* (e-mag., #48): Lightspeed Magazine, May 2014.

(r) *The Right Way to be Crippled and Naked: The Fiction of Disability* (anth., ed. Sheila Black, Michael Northen, and Annabelle Hayse): Cinco Puntos Press, 2017.

(c) *Filter House* (f.c.): Aqueduct Press, 2008.

"Down in the Flood"

(1) *Daughters of Nyx* (mag., #7): Ruby Rose's Fairy Tale Emporium, Summer/Fall 1996.

(r) *Pangaia* (mag., #16): BBI Media, Summer 1998.

(r) *PodCastle, Miniature* (podcast/ audio, #31): Escape Artists, Inc., May 2009.

"Dynamo Hum"

(1) *Afro-Future Females: Black Writers Chart Science Fiction's Newest New Wave Trajectory* (anth., ed. Marleen S. Barr): Ohio State University Press, 2008.

"Extremiades"

(1) *Like a Coming Wave: Oceanic Erotica* (anth., ed. Cecilia Tan and Andrea Trask): Circlet Press, 2012.

"The Five Petals of Thought"

(1) *Missing Links and Secret Histories: A Selection of Wikipedia Entries from Across the Known Multiverse* (anth., ed. L. Timmel Duchamp): Aqueduct Press, 2013.

"Good Boy" (novelette)

(c) *Filter House* (f.c.): Aqueduct Press, 2008.

(r) *Alas!* (online media): amptoons.com, Dec. 2009.

(r) *Mothership: Tales from Afrofuturism and Beyond* (anth., ed. Edward Austin Hall and Bill Campbell): Rosarium Publishing, 2013.

(r) *The Mammoth Book of SF Stories by Women* (anth., ed. Alex Dally MacFarlane): Running Press/ Robinson, 2014.

"Honorary Earthling"

(1) *Expanded Horizons* (e-mag., #33): expandedhorizons.net, Dec. 2011.

(r) *Aliens: Recent Encounters* (anth., ed. Alex Dally MacFarlane): Prime Books, 2013.

"I Was a Teenage Genetic Engineer" (as Denise Angela Shawl)

(1) *Semiotext[e] SF* (anth., ed. Rudy Rucker, Peter Lamborn Wilson, and Robert Anton Wilson): Autonomedia, 1989.

"In Blood and Song" (with Michael Ehart)

(1) *Dark Faith: Invocations* (anth., ed. Jerry Gordon and Maurice Broaddus): Apex Publications, 2012.

"In Colors Everywhere"

(1) *The Other Half of the Sky* (anth., ed. Athena Andreadis and Kay Holt): Candlemark & Gleam, 2013.

(r) *How to Live on Other Planets: A Handbook for Aspiring Aliens* (anth., ed. Joanne Merriam): Upper Rubber Boot Books, 2015.

"Jamaica Ginger" (with Nalo Hopkinson)

(1) *Stories for Chip: A Tribute to Samuel R. Delany* (anth., ed. Nisi Shawl and Bill Campbell): Rosarium Publishing, 2015.

(r) *The Best Science Fiction and Fantasy of the Year: Volume Ten* (anth., ed. Jonathan Strahan): Solaris, 2016.

"Just Between Us"

(1) *Phantom Drift, A Journal of New Fabulism* (mag., #1): Phantom Drift Limited, Fall 2011.

(r) *Hex Publishers* (online media): hexpublishers.com, Dec. 2016.

(c) *Exploring Dark Short Fiction #3: A Primer to Nisi Shawl* (f.c., ed. Eric J. Guignard): Dark Moon Books, 2018.

"Lazzrus"

(1) *Upside Down: Inverted Tropes in Storytelling* (anth., ed. Jaym Gates and Monica L. Valentinelli): Apex Publications, 2016.

"Like the Deadly Hands"

(1) *Analog Science Fiction and Fact* (mag., v.86, #12): Dell Magazines, Dec. 2016.

"Little Horses"

(1) *Detroit Noir* (anth., ed. E.J. Olsen and John C. Hocking): Akashic Books, 2007.

(c) *Filter House* (f.c.): Aqueduct Press, 2008.

"Looking for Lilith"

(1) *Lenox Avenue* (mag., #1): Lenox Avenue Magazine, Jul. 2004.

(r) *Choose Wisely: 35 Women Up To No Good* (anth., ed. H. L. Nelson and Joanne Merriam): Upper Rubber Boot Books, 2015.

"Luisah's Church"
(1) *Dark Discoveries* (mag., #36): Dark Discoveries Publications/ JournalStone, Fall 2016.
(r) *Apex Magazine* (mag., #108): Apex Publications, May 2018.

"Lupine"
(1) *Once Upon a Time: New Fairy Tales* (anth., ed. Paula Guran): Prime Books, 2013.

"Maggies"
(1) *Dark Matter: Reading the Bones* (anth., ed. Sheree R. Thomas): Aspect/ Warner Books, 2004.
(c) *Filter House* (f.c.): Aqueduct Press, 2008.

"Matched"
(1) *The Infinite Matrix* (e-mag.): The Infinite Matrix, May 2005.

"The Mighty Phin"
(1) *Cyber World: Tales of Humanity's Tomorrow* (anth., ed. Joshua Viola and Jason Heller): Hex Publishers, 2016.
(r) *Tor.com* (online media): tor.com, Jun. 2016.

"Momi Watu"
(1) *Strange Horizons* (online media): strangehorizons.com, Aug. 2003.
(c) *Filter House* (f.c.): Aqueduct Press, 2008.

"More than Nothing"
(1) *Tor.com* (online media): tor.com, Mar. 2017.

"New Action"
(1) *e-flux* (online media): e-flux.com, Sep. 2018.

"Otherwise"
(1) *Brave New Love: 15 Dystopian Tales of Desire* (anth., ed. Paula Guran): Running Press, 2012.

(r) *Heiresses of Russ 2013: The Year's Best Lesbian Speculative Fiction* (anth., ed. Tenea D. Johnson and Steve Berman): Lethe Press, 2013.

(c) *Exploring Dark Short Fiction #3: A Primer to Nisi Shawl* (f.c., ed. Eric J. Guignard): Dark Moon Books, 2018.

"**P**ataki (Part 1 of 2)"

(1) *Strange Horizons* (online media): strangehorizons.com, Apr., 2011.

(c) *Something More and More* (f.c.): Aqueduct Press, 2011.

"**P**ataki (Part 2 of 2)"

(1) *Strange Horizons* (online media): strangehorizons.com, Apr., 2011.

(c) *Something More and More* (f.c.): Aqueduct Press, 2011.

"The **P**ragmatical Princess"

(1) *Asimov's Science Fiction* (mag., v.23, #1): Dell Magazines, Jan. 1999.

(r) *Fantasy Magazine* (mag., #53): Prime Books, Aug. 2011.

(c) *Filter House* (f.c.): Aqueduct Press, 2008.

"**P**romised"

(1) *Steampunk World* (anth., ed. Sarah Hans): Alliteration Ink, 2014.

"**Q**ueen of Dirt"

(1) *Apex Magazine* (e-mag., #93): Apex Publications, Feb. 2017.

"The **R**ainses'" (var: The Raineses')

(1) *Asimov's Science Fiction* (mag., v.19, #4/5): Bantam Doubleday Dell Magazines, Apr. 1995.

(r) *Isaac Asimov's Ghosts* (anth., ed. Sheila Williams and Gardner Dozois): Ace Books, 1995.

(c) *Filter House* (f.c.): Aqueduct Press, 2008.

"**R**ed Matty"

(1) *Strange Horizons* (online media): strangehorizons.com, Sep. 2013.

"The Return of Chérie"

(1) *Steam-Powered II: More Lesbian Steampunk Stories* (anth., ed. JoSelle Vanderhooft): Torquere Press, 2011.

(r) *The Mammoth Book of Steampunk Adventures* (anth., ed. Sean Wallace): Running Press/ Robinson, 2014.

"Salt on the Dance Floor"

(1) *Beast Within 3: Oceans Unleashed* (anth., ed. Jennifer Brozek): Graveside Tales, 2012.

(r) *Not Your Average Monster, Vol. 2: A Menagerie of Vile Beasts* (anth., ed. Pete Kahle): Bloodshot Books, 2016.

"Shiomah's Land"

(1) *Asimov's Science Fiction* (mag., v.25, #3): Dell Magazines, Mar. 2001.

(r) *Clarkesworld.com* (e-mag., #133): clarkesworld.com, Oct. 2017.

(c) *Filter House* (f.c.): Aqueduct Press, 2008.

"Slippernet"

(1) *Slate Magazine* (online media): slate.com, Feb. 2017.

"The Snooted One: The Historicity of Origin"

(1) *Farrago's Wainscot* (e-mag., #1): Farrago's Wainscot, Jan. 2007.

"Something More" (novelette)

(c) *Something More and More* (f.c.): Aqueduct Press, 2011.

"Street Worm"

(1) *Streets of Shadows* (anth., ed. Maurice Broaddus and Jerry Gordon): Alliteration Ink, 2014.

(r) *Street Magicks* (anth., ed. Paula Guran): Prime Books, 2016.

(c) *Exploring Dark Short Fiction #3: A Primer to Nisi Shawl* (f.c., ed. Eric J. Guignard): Dark Moon Books, 2018.

"Sun River"

(1) *Clockwork Cairo: Steampunk Tales of Egypt* (anth., ed. Matthew Bright): Twopenny Books, 2017.

"Sunshine of Your Love"

(1) *The Sum of Us: Tales of the Bonded and Bound* (anth., ed. Susan Forest and Lucas K. Law): Laksa Media Groups Inc., 2017.

"The Tawny Bitch"

(1) *Mojo: Conjure Stories* (anth., ed. Nalo Hopkinson): Aspect/ Warner Books, 2003.

(r) *The Mammoth Book of Gaslit Romance* (anth., ed. Ekaterina Sedia): Running Press/ Robinson, 2014.

"The Third Petal"

(1) *Wired Magazine* (online media): wired.com, Dec. 2018.

"To the Moment"

(1) *Reflection's Edge* (e-mag.): Reflection's Edge, Nov. 2007.

(r) *Vampires: The Recent Undead* (anth., ed. Paula Guran): Prime Books, 2011.

"Vapors"

(1) *Wet: More Aqua Erotica* (anth., ed. Mary Anne Mohanraj): Three Rivers Press, 2002.

"Vulcanization"

(1) *Nightmare Magazine* (online media): nightmare-mag.com, Jan. 2016

"Walk Like a Man"

(1) *Bahamut* (mag., #1): Underland Press, Jun. 2015.

"Wallamelon" (novelette)

(1) *Aeon* (mag., #3): Scorpius Digital Publishing, May. 2005.

(r) *Magic City: Recent Spells* (anth., ed. Paula Guran): Prime Books, 2014.

(r) *Far Fetched Fables* (podcast/ audio, #154): District of Wonders, Apr. 2017.

(c) *Filter House* (f.c.): Aqueduct Press, 2008.

"The Water Museum"

(c) *Filter House* (f.c.): Aqueduct Press, 2008.

(r) *Alas!* (online media): amptoons.com, Dec. 2009.

(r) *Telling Tales: The Clarion West 30th Anniversary Anthology* (anth., ed. Ellen Datlow): Hydra House, 2013.

"White Dawn"

(1) *Athena's Daughters: Women in Science Fiction & Fantasy, vol. 1* (anth., ed. Jean Rabe): Silence in the Library, 2014.

(r) *Procyon Press Science Fiction Anthology 2016* (anth., ed. Jeanne Thornton): Procyon Press/ Tayen Lane, 2016.

"Women of the Doll"

(1) *Greatest Uncommon Denominator* (e-mag., #1): Greatest Uncommon Denominator Publishing, Autumn 2007.

"Wonder-Worker-of-the-World"

(1) *Reflection's Edge* (e-mag.): Reflection's Edge, May 2005.

NOVELS, CHAPBOOKS, and OTHER SINGLE WORKS

Everfair (novel): Tor, 2016.

COLLECTIONS

Exploring Dark Short Fiction #3: A Primer to Nisi Shawl (fiction collection, ed. Eric J. Guignard): Dark Moon Books, 2018.

Filter House (fiction collection): Aqueduct Press, 2008.

Something More and More (fiction collection): Aqueduct Press, 2011.

ANTHOLOGIES AS EDITOR

Bloodchildren: Stories by the Octavia E. Butler Scholars: Book View Café, 2013.

Stories for Chip: A Tribute to Samuel R. Delany (with Bill Campbell): Rosarium Publishing, 2015.

Strange Matings: Science Fiction, Feminism, African American Voices, and Octavia E. Butler (with Rebecca J. Holden): Aqueduct Press, 2013.

The WisCon Chronicles, Vol.5: Writing and Racial Identity: Aqueduct Press, 2011.

Writing the Other: A Practical Approach (with Cynthia Ward): Aqueduct Press, 2005.

MAGAZINES AS EDITOR

Fantastic Stories of the Imagination (e-mag., People of Color Take Over: Special Issue): Positronic Publishing, Jun. 2017.

Lightspeed Magazine (e-mag., People of Colo(u)r Destroy Science Fiction!: Special Issue): Lightspeed Magazine, Jun. 2016.

Obsidian (mag., Special Speculative Fiction Double-Volume Issue #42.1 and 42.2): Illinois State University, Fall 2016.

ALSO FROM ERIC J. GUIGNARD AND DARK MOON BOOKS:

Every nation of the globe has unique tales to tell, whispers that settle in through the land, creatures or superstitions that enliven the night, but rarely do readers get to experience such a diversity of these voices in one place as in ***A WORLD OF HORROR***, the latest anthology book created by award-winning editor Eric J. Guignard, and beautifully illustrated by artist Steve Lines.

Enclosed within its pages are twenty-two all-new dark and speculative fiction stories written by authors from around the world that explore the myths and monsters, fables and fears of their homelands.

Encounter the haunting things that stalk those radioactive forests outside Chernobyl in Ukraine; sample the curious dishes one may eat in Canada; beware the veldt monster that mirrors yourself in Uganda; or simply battle mountain trolls alongside Alfred Nobel in Sweden. These stories and more are found within *A World of Horror*: Enter and discover, truly, there's no place on the planet devoid of frights, thrills, and wondrous imagination.

"This breath of fresh air for horror readers shows the limitless possibilities of the genre."

—*Publishers Weekly* (starred review)

"A fresh collection of horror authors exploring monsters and myths from their homelands."

—*Library Journal*

Order your copy at www.darkmoonbooks.com or www.amazon.com

ISBN-13: 978-0-9989383-1-8

ALSO FROM ERIC J. GUIGNARD AND DARK MOON BOOKS:

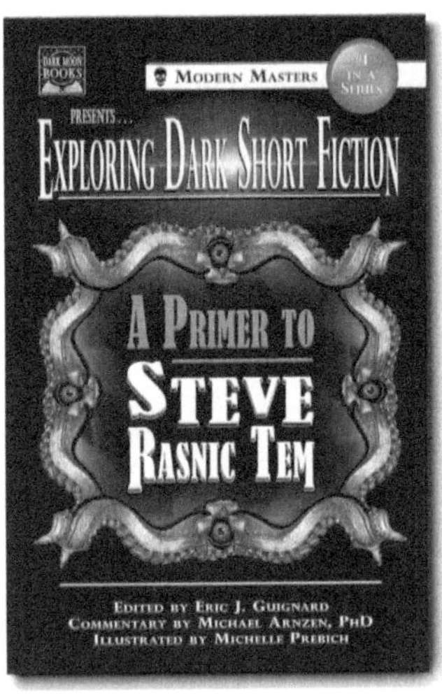

Exploring Dark Short Fiction #1: A Primer to Steve Rasnic Tem

For over four decades, Steve Rasnic Tem has been an acclaimed author of horror, weird, and sentimental fiction. Hailed by *Publishers Weekly* as "A perfect balance between the bizarre and the straight-forward" and *Library Journal* as "One of the most distinctive voices in imaginative literature," Steve Rasnic Tem has been read and cherished the world over for his affecting, genre-crossing tales.

Dark Moon Books and editor Eric J. Guignard bring you this introduction to his work, the first in a series of primers exploring modern masters of literary dark short fiction. Herein is a chance to discover—or learn more of—the rich voice of Steve Rasnic Tem, as beautifully illustrated by artist Michelle Prebich.

Included within these pages are:

- Six short stories, one written exclusively for this book
- Author interview
- Complete bibliography
- Academic commentary by Michael Arnzen, PhD (former humanities chair and professor of the year, Seton Hill University)
- . . . and more!

Enter this doorway to the vast and fantastic: Get to know Steve Rasnic Tem.

Order your copy at www.darkmoonbooks.com or www.amazon.com
ISBN-13: 978-0-9885569-2-8

ALSO FROM ERIC J. GUIGNARD AND DARK MOON BOOKS:

Exploring Dark Short Fiction #2: A Primer to Kaaron Warren

Australian author Kaaron Warren is widely recognized as one of the leading writers today of speculative and dark short fiction. She's published four novels, multiple novellas, and well over one hundred heart-rending tales of horror, science fiction, and beautiful fantasy, and is the first author ever to simultaneously win all three of Australia's top speculative fiction writing awards (Ditmar, Shadows, and Aurealis awards for *The Grief Hole*).

Dark Moon Books and editor Eric J. Guignard bring you this introduction to her work, the second in a series of primers exploring modern masters of literary dark short fiction. Herein is a chance to discover—or learn more of—the distinct voice of Kaaron Warren, as beautifully illustrated by artist Michelle Prebich.

Included within these pages are:

- Six short stories, one written exclusively for this book
- Author interview
- Complete bibliography
- Academic commentary by Michael Arnzen, PhD (former humanities chair and professor of the year, Seton Hill University)
- . . . and more!

Enter this doorway to the vast and fantastic: Get to know Kaaron Warren.

Order your copy at www.darkmoonbooks.com or www.amazon.com

ISBN-13: 978-0-9989383-0-1

ALSO FROM ERIC J. GUIGNARD AND DARK MOON BOOKS:

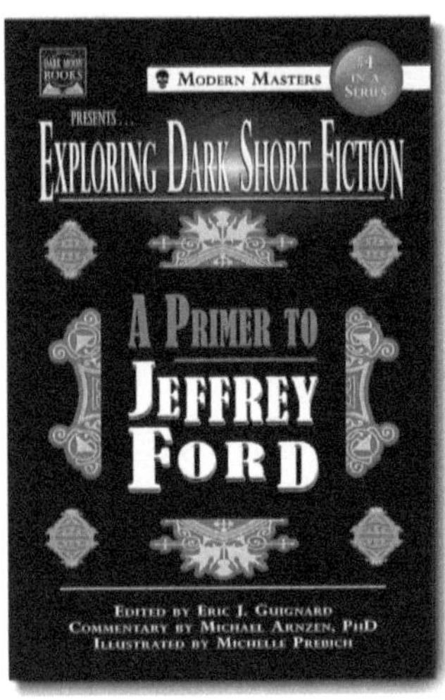

Exploring Dark Short Fiction #4:
A Primer to Jeffrey Ford

Author of the fantastic and the bizarre, Jeffrey Ford's work has won awards and acclaim across the globe for his stories of humor, horror, and unconventional beauty. "Powerful and disturbing in the best possible way" (*Gawker*) and "Intensely engaging" (*Publishers Weekly*), Ford crosses speculative genres with literary ideals, which has earned him the World Fantasy Award (seven times), the Shirley Jackson Award (four times), the Edgar Allan Poe Award, and France's vaunted *Grand Prix de l'Imaginaire*.

Dark Moon Books and editor Eric J. Guignard bring you this introduction to his work, the fourth in a series of primers exploring modern masters of literary dark short fiction. Herein is a chance to discover—or learn more of—the extraordinary voice of Jeffrey Ford, as beautifully illustrated by artist Michelle Prebich.

Included within these pages are:

- Six short stories, one written exclusively for this book
- Author interview
- Complete bibliography
- Academic commentary by Michael Arnzen, PhD (former humanities chair and professor of the year, Seton Hill University)
- . . . and more!

Enter this doorway to the vast and fantastic: Get to know Jeffrey Ford.

Order your copy at www.darkmoonbooks.com or www.amazon.com
ISBN-13: 978-0-9989383-8-7

ALSO FROM ERIC J. GUIGNARD AND DARK MOON BOOKS:

Exploring Dark Short Fiction #5: A Primer to Han Song

Considered one of the three most important voices in contemporary Chinese science fiction, Han Song is a multiple recipient of the Chinese Galaxy Award, as well as the Chinese Nebula Award and Asian-Pacific Sci-fi Gravity Award. Song bridges new developments in science and subjects of cultural and social dynamics with "absurdly dark" stories of dystopia, governmental conspiracy, and subversive horror.

Including original English translations by Nathaniel Isaacson, PhD, Dark Moon Books and editor Eric J. Guignard bring you this introduction to Han Song's work, the fifth in a series of primers exploring modern masters of literary dark short fiction. Herein is a chance to discover—or learn more of—the enigmatic voice of Han Song, as beautifully illustrated by artist Michelle Prebich.

Included within these pages are:

- Six short stories, three translated exclusively for this book
- Author interview
- Complete bibliography
- Academic commentary by Michael Arnzen, PhD (former humanities chair and professor of the year, Seton Hill University)
- . . . and more!

Enter this doorway to the vast and fantastic: Get to know Han Song.

Order your copy at www.darkmoonbooks.com or www.amazon.com
ISBN-13: 978-1-949491-12-8

ALSO FROM ERIC J. GUIGNARD AND DARK MOON BOOKS:

Pop the Clutch: Thrilling Tales of Rockabilly, Monsters, and Hot Rod Horror

Welcome to the cool side of the 1950s, where the fast cars and revved-up movie monsters peel out in the night. Where outlaw vixens and jukebox tramps square off with razorblades and lead pipes. Where rockers rock, cool cats strut, and hot rods roar. Where you howl to the moon as the tiki drums pound and the electric guitar shrieks and that spit-and-holler jamboree ain't gonna stop for a long, long time . . . maybe never.

This is the '50s where ghost shows still travel the back roads of the south, and rockabilly has a hold on the nation's youth; where lucky hearts tell the tale, and maybe that fella in the Shriners' fez ain't so square after all. Where exist noir detectives of the supernatural, tattoo artists of another kind, Hollywood fix-it men, and a punk kid with grasshopper arms under his chain-studded jacket and an icy stare on his face.

This is the '50s of *Pop the Clutch: Thrilling Tales of Rockabilly, Monsters, and Hot Rod Horror*. This is your ticket to the dark side of American kitsch . . . the fun and frightful side!

"A fitting tribute to the 1950s with this 18-story compendium of hot rods, rock 'n' roll, and creature features come to life."

—*Publishers Weekly*

Order your copy at www.darkmoonbooks.com or www.amazon.com

ISBN-13: 978-0-9834335-9-0

ALSO FROM ERIC J. GUIGNARD AND DARK MOON BOOKS:

Death. Who has not considered their own mortality and wondered at what awaits, once our frail human shell expires? What occurs after the heart stops beating, after the last breath is drawn, after life as we know it terminates?

Does our spirit remain on Earth while the body rots? Do the remnants of our soul transcend to a celestial Heaven or sink to Hell's torment? Can we choose our own afterlife? Can we die again in the hereafter? Are we given the opportunity to reincarnate and do it all over? Is life merely a cosmic joke or is it an experiment for something greater? Enclosed in this Bram Stoker-award winning anthology are thirty-four all-new dark and speculative fiction stories exploring the possibilities ***AFTER DEATH*** . . .

"Though the majority of the pieces come from the darker side of the genre, a solid minority are playful, clever, or full of wonder. This strong and well-themed anthology is sure to make readers contemplative even while it creates nightmares."

—*Publishers Weekly*

"In Eric J. Guignard's latest anthology he gathers some of the biggest and most talented authors on the planet to give us their take on this entertaining and perplexing subject matter . . . highly recommended."

—*Famous Monsters of Filmland*

"An excellent collection of imaginative tales of what waits beyond the veil."

—*Amazing Stories Magazine*

Order your copy at www.darkmoonbooks.com or www.amazon.com

ISBN-13: 978-0-9885569-2-8

ALSO FROM ERIC J. GUIGNARD AND DARK MOON BOOKS:

In this anthology, ***DARK TALES OF LOST CIVILIZATIONS***, you will unearth twenty-five previously unpublished horror and speculative fiction stories relating to aspects of civilizations that are crumbling, forgotten, rediscovered, or perhaps merely spoken about in great and fearful whispers.

What is it that lures explorers to distant lands where none have returned? Where is Genghis Khan buried? What happened to Atlantis? Who will displace mankind on Earth? What laments have the Witches of Oz? Answers to these mysteries and other tales are presented within this critically acclaimed anthology.

"The stories range from mildly disturbing to downright terrifying... Most are written in a conservative, suggestive style, relying on the reader's own imagination to take the plunge from speculation to horror."

—*Monster Librarian Reviews*

"Several of these stories made it on to my best of the year shortlist, and the book itself is now on the best anthologies of the year shortlist."

—*British Fantasy Society*

"Almost any story in this anthology is worth the price of purchase. The entire collection is a delight."

—*Black Gate Magazine*

Order your copy at www.darkmoonbooks.com or www.amazon.com

ISBN-13: 978-0-9834335-9-0

ALSO FROM ERIC J. GUIGNARD AND DARK MOON BOOKS:

Hearing, sight, touch, smell, and taste: Our impressions of the world are formed by our five senses, and so too are our fears, our imaginations, and our captivation in reading fiction stories that embrace these senses.

Whether hearing the song of infernal caverns, tasting the erotic kiss of treachery, or smelling the lush fragrance of a fiend, enclosed within this anthology are fifteen horror and dark fantasy tales that will quicken the beat of fear, sweeten the flavor of wonder, sharpen the spike of thrills, and otherwise brighten the marvel of storytelling that is found resonant!

Editor Eric J. Guignard and psychologist Jessica Bayliss, PhD also include companion discourse throughout, offering academic and literary insight as well as psychological commentary examining the physiology of our senses, why each of our senses are engaged by dark fiction stories, and how it all inspires writers to continually churn out ideas in uncommon and invigorating ways.

Featuring stunning interior illustrations by Nils Bross, and including fiction short stories by such world-renowned authors as John Farris, Ramsey Campbell, Poppy Z. Brite, Darrell Schweitzer, and Richard Christian Matheson, amongst others.

Intended for readers, writers, and students alike, explore ***THE FIVE SENSES OF HORROR***!

Order your copy at www.darkmoonbooks.com or www.amazon.com

ISBN-13: 978-0-9988275-0-6

THE CRIME FILES OF KATY GREEN by GENE O'NEILL:

Discover why readers have been applauding this stark, fast-paced noir series by multiple-award-winning author, Gene O'Neill, and follow the dark murder mysteries of Sacramento homicide detectives Katy Green and Johnny Cato, dubbed by the press as Sacramento's "Green Hornet and Cato"!

Book #1: DOUBLE JACK (a novella)

400-pound serial killer Jack Malenko has discovered the perfect cover: He dresses as a CalTrans worker and preys on female motorists in distress in full sight of passing traffic. How fast can Katy Green and Johnny Cato track him down before he strikes again?

Book #2: SHADOW OF THE DARK ANGEL

Bullied misfit, Samuel Kubiak, is visited by a dark guardian angel who helps Samuel gain just vengeance. There hasn't been a case yet Katy and Johnny haven't solved, but now how can they track a psychopathic suspect that comes and goes in the shadows?

Book #3: DEATHFLASH

Billy Williams can see the soul as it departs the body, and is "commanded to do the Lord's work," which he does fanatically, slaying drug addicts in San Francisco . . . Katy and Johnny investigate the case as junkies die all around, for Billy has his own addiction: the rush of viewing the Deathflash.

Order your copy at www.darkmoonbooks.com or www.amazon.com

ALSO FROM GENE O'NEILL AND DARK MOON BOOKS:

A STICK OF DOUBLEMINT

—Book #4 in the series, ***THE CRIME FILES OF KATY GREEN***

On a warm San Francisco night, an innocent young woman is gunned down in a gang-related drive-by shooting. The overworked police department have no leads and no suspects, and seemingly little interest in pursuing yet another case involving ongoing gang violence. Then those involved in the shooting start turning up dead, with a stick of Doublemint gum in hand. What does it mean, and who's responsible?

A new detective is assigned to the case, and he quickly realizes he's going to need help to solve it, so turns to old friends, Katy Green and Johnny Cato, now part of a successful private investigation firm!

So begins a race against the clock to stop further murders and to discover the perpetrator. Can the investigating duo, dubbed by newspapers as "Green Hornet and Cato" solve this latest case of the vigilante killings, or will the culprit continue to bloody the city?

Read ***A STICK OF DOUBLEMINT*** and then continue the shocking case files of Sacramento's "Green Hornet and Cato" with volumes 1–3 (*Double Jack*; *Shadow of the Dark Angel*; and *Deathflash*).

Order your copy at www.darkmoonbooks.com or www.amazon.com

ISBN-13: 978-1-949491-18-0

About Editor, Eric J. Guignard

ERIC J. GUIGNARD IS A writer and editor of dark and speculative fiction, operating from the shadowy outskirts of Los Angeles, where he also runs the small press Dark Moon Books. He's twice won the Bram Stoker Award (the highest literary award of horror fiction), been a finalist for the International Thriller Writers Award, and a multi-nominee of the Pushcart Prize.

He has over one hundred stories and non-fiction author credits appearing in publications around the world. As editor, Eric's published multiple fiction anthologies, including his most recent, *Pop the Clutch: Thrilling Tales of Rockabilly, Monsters, and Hot Rod Horror*; and *A World of Horror*, a showcase of international horror short fiction.

He currently publishes the acclaimed series of author primers created to champion modern masters of the dark and macabre: *Exploring Dark Short Fiction* (*Vol. 1: Steve Rasnic Tem*; *Vol. II: Kaaron Warren*; *Vol. III: Nisi Shawl*; *Vol. IV: Jeffrey Ford*; *Vol. V: Han Song*; *Vol. VI: Ramsey Campbell)*. Additionally he curates the series, *The Horror Writers Association Presents: Haunted Library of Horror Classics* through SourceBooks with co-editor Leslie S. Klinger.

His latest books are his novel *Doorways to the Deadeye* and short story collection *That Which Grows Wild: 16 Tales of Dark Fiction* (Cemetery Dance).

Outside the glamorous and jet-setting world of indie fiction, Eric's a technical writer and college professor, and he stumbles home each day to a wife, children, dogs, and a terrarium filled with mischievous beetles. Visit Eric at: www.ericjguignard.com, his blog: ericjguignard.blogspot.com, or Twitter: @ericjguignard.

About Academic, Michael Arnzen, PhD

MICHAEL A. ARNZEN (PhD, University of Oregon, 1999) teaches full-time at Seton Hill University, home of the country's only MFA degree in Writing Popular Fiction. To date he has won four Bram Stoker Awards and an International Horror Critics Guild Award for his often funny, always disturbing horror fiction and poetry, which includes such book-length titles as *Grave Markings*, *Play Dead*, *Freakcidents*, and *Proverbs for Monsters*. Alongside Heidi Ruby Miller, Arnzen also co-edited *Many Genres, One Craft: Lessons in Writing Popular Fiction*—a large how-to guide for authors of speculative fiction and other genres. Arnzen continues to write horror and criticism while teaching the zombie populations near Pittsburgh, PA. Follow Mike at http://michaelarnzen.com.

On top of his genre writing, Arnzen sits on the editorial board for *Paradoxa: Studies in World Literary Genres*, and his academic criticism has appeared in such journals as *Narrative*, *The Journal of Popular Film and Television*, and the *Journal of the Fantastic in the Arts*. An updated version of his doctoral dissertation—a critical survey of Freud's "unheimlich" in pop culture, called *The Popular Uncanny*—is forthcoming from Guide Dog Books. He maintains an irregular blog on the subject at http://gorelets.com/uncanny.

About Illustrator, Michelle Prebich

MICHELLE PREBICH IS A freelance artist who studied Film Production, Theatre, and Fine Art at Cal-State Long Beach. A film and literature geek, she loves the dark/romantic era and existential themes.

She has worked as a production designer, artist, set dresser, property master, and special effects makeup artist on short films, television segments, and web series for the film industry. Her collaboration with the band *Mr. Moonshine* includes art for their album and direction/design on two stop motion animation music videos. Her art he has been featured in galleries including Melt Down Comics and The Mystic Museum.

She sells original macabre art, art pieces, and apparel she has created through her shop "Bat in Your Belfry," which can be found at batinyourbelfry.etsy.com and on Instagram @batinyourbelfry. She loves geeking out with fellow enthusiasts of the unusual and macabre and can be typically found at Halloween/horror conventions usually standing next to a man in a cowboy hat.

www.ingramcontent.com/pod-product-compliance
Lightning Source LLC
Chambersburg PA
CBHW030610310726
48979CB00003B/639
* 9 7 8 1 9 4 9 4 9 1 0 9 8 *